# TUCKER

# TUCKER

## Tom Birdseye

Holiday House / New York

Library of Congress Cataloging-in-Publication Data

Birdseye, Tom.
    Tucker / written by Tom Birdseye. — 1st ed.
        p.      cm.
    Summary: Eleven-year-old Tucker likes his life with his divorced father,
until the nine-year-old sister he has not seen in years moves back in with
them and claims that their mother wants them to become one family again.
    ISBN 0-8234-0813-2
    [1. Brothers and sisters—Fiction.    2. Single-parent family—Fiction.
3. Divorce—Fiction.]    I. Title.
PZ7.B5213Tu    1990
[Fic]—dc20        89-46243        CIP        AC

*For Dad, Mom, Ann, and Mark—together,
and with thanks to Deb, Eli, Tim, and the kids,
and to Margery Cuyler, editor fantástico*

# TUCKER

# 1

The bear is asleep. It is lying on its side in the late summer sun like a huge shaggy dog. I can hear it breathe—in and out, in and out. The sound covers the mountainside as if the boulders and pines themselves are alive. I stand very still, my breath shallow, silent as it crosses my dry lips.

The breeze picks up again. The bear's fur moves, the hairs standing up like soldiers on guard. They glow the color of cinnamon in the sun, except on the ends, which are silver. My heartbeat quickens. It is a grizzly that I stalk.

Slowly, more so than all the braves who have stalked and touched sleeping bears before me, I lift one foot and move it forward. I do not take my eyes *from the bear. If it wakes it will descend on me with the angry speed of a clap of thunder. There will be no time to run away or climb a tree. I have no weapon. I must touch my foot to the ground in rhythm with the natural sounds of the forest. It must come to rest so gently and evenly that no twig snaps, no stone turns, as if my toes have eyes.*

*Now I move the other foot forward, crouching low as I approach the bear. Elders wait at the village for me, sending out their prayers for my success in this test of skill and bravery. They remember when they too stalked the bear. They can still feel the coarseness of its fur on their fingertips. They have always carried the day that they became a man very close in their hearts. I will do the same.*

*The pungent smell of the sleeping bear suddenly reaches my nostrils. I am only three, no, maybe four steps away. There is no turning back. I must keep my mind clear. Noisy thoughts would wake him as surely as noisy feet. I take a deep, slow breath and hold it. I move silently forward and reach out my hand, stretching through the shortening distance between human and beast, hunter and hunter. Balancing my life on my fingertips, I will now . . . touch . . . the bear—*

"Tucker, she's here."

*I will now . . . touch . . . the bear—*

"Olivia's flight just arrived at gate three. She'll be getting off the plane in just a minute."

*—and begin my passage into the man's world of The Tribe.*

A hand came to rest on Tucker Renfro's shoulder. "It's your sister. She's here!"

Tucker pressed his nose against the glass and looked one more time at the stuffed grizzly bear inside the large showcase. Travelers moved around him on the red concourse of the Spokane International Airport as if he were a rock in a stream. The glass eyes of the bear stared out at them in fierce defiance. Tucker felt the same way. He blew a circle of breath onto the bear's glass case.

The hand on his shoulder squeezed gently. "C'mon, son, let's go welcome Olivia to the Northwest."

Tucker turned and looked up at his father. The two mirrored one another in many ways: brown hair, high cheekbones, slender build, and a particular look in the green eyes, as if often thinking of distant places, other things. Father and son. Most people saw it right away. "But, Dad, I don't even know her," Tucker said.

Duane Renfro tried to smile. "That's the whole point. Your mother and I never intended to let things go . . ." He stopped and looked down the concourse toward gate three, then took a deep breath. ". . . go this long. Seven years is seven too many. You were only four when we split up. Olivia was only two."

Tucker stuck his hands down deep in his pockets. In the left one the small piece of cedar root he had carved into an Indian chief's head slipped comfortably into his hand, as if it had always been there. He ran his fingers across the face, then back over the war bonnet of carved eagle feathers. He had spent hours working on it. "Why change things now, Dad?" he asked. "We get along OK by ourselves."

An instant of pain flashed across his father's green eyes. "Just because your mother and I are divorced, that doesn't erase the fact that you and Olivia are brother and sister. She will be able to start the school year with you here—her in fourth grade and you in sixth. Be thankful that your mother and I have finally been able to agree on something and bring you two together, even if only until Thanksgiving."

Tucker turned and pressed his nose against the glass case again. A brass plaque was mounted at the bear's feet: WORLD RECORD CLASS GRIZZLY BEAR. SHOT BY SCOTT GRAHAM OF SPOKANE, WASHINGTON, IN BRITISH COLUMBIA, CANADA, 1988. TAXIDERMY BY KNOPP BROTHERS. HUNT ARRANGED BY WORLDWIDE TROPHY OUTFITTERS, SPOKANE, WASHINGTON.

"They've opened the door at gate three, Tucker," his father's voice came over his shoulder. "Please try to be open-minded and give it a chance. According to your mother it was Olivia who first brought this up. She really wants to be here and to get to know you. It probably wouldn't be happening if she hadn't insisted."

Tucker looked once more into the fierce glass eyes of the grizzly bear. *I have stalked the bear as it sleeps. By completing this test of bravery, I begin my passage into the man's world of The Tribe—*

"There she is, Tucker." His father's excited voice cut in once again. "Just like in the picture your mother sent. I can see her coming up the ramp!"

*—and become a warrior.*

# 2

"You want to play Slug Bug?"

The face that leaned over the backseat of Duane Renfro's white station wagon had a smile on it that stretched from ear to ear. Large brown eyes sparkled. Sandy blond hair was cut straight across the front into bangs, the rest pulled back into a ponytail that fell onto a pink-and-lime-green T-shirt with a picture on it of two elephants riding a surfboard.

Tucker ignored his sister, keeping his eyes on the line of white dashes down the middle of the road that stretched out ahead toward Sandpoint, Idaho.

"It's a great game, really," Olivia insisted. "Every time you see one of those little old Volkswagen Beetle cars you yell 'Slug Bug!' and the one who yells it

8

first gets to slug the other players in the arm. Mom says she used to play it with Uncle Stanley when she was a girl."

Duane Renfro laughed softly and looked in the rearview mirror at his daughter. "It sure is good to have you here, Olivia," he said for the third time.

She smiled, again wide enough to touch both ears. "Just call me Livi. That's what Mom calls me, all my friends back in Kentucky, too. I'll bet your friends here call you Tuck, huh, brother?"

Tucker blew out a puff of air. "No," he said, still looking straight ahead. *I am a warrior. I have stalked the bear.*

Livi seemed not to notice the edge in his voice. "Well, Tucker, I keep my mouth ready to yell 'Slug Bug!' when I play the Slug Bug game." She leaned over even farther and twisted her face around in an attempt to get in Tucker's view. "See, my mouth is ready to yell 'Slug Bug!' "

Just then a logging truck passed, its load towering over the small station wagon.

Livi's eyes went wide. "Wow! Look at the size of those logs!"

Duane Renfro shook his head. "Old growth timber. Those trees could be up to two hundred years old or more. They'll soon be plywood, Olivia—"

"Livi."

He checked the rearview mirror again and

smiled. "Sorry, Livi, I can't get used to calling you that. I remember you only as a Kentucky two-year-old named Olivia who hugged me like a bear when I came home from teaching." He looked back at the log truck. "I can't get used to seeing those big trees on their deathbed, either. We should be leaving them for people to enjoy standing tall. That's why I won't work at the mill."

Tucker looked sidelong at his father, then out the window. The first hint of fall could be seen in the clumps of birch and aspen beside the road. *A warrior should provide for his people. That is his work, no matter what.* In the distance the twin peaks of Butler and Blacktail Mountain were now in view, their rocky tops pushing up and away from dark evergreen flanks. *I will go to the place of The Tribe.* The two-hour ride was almost over. It was only six more miles to home.

Livi was going on about the logs on the truck again— "They're so BIG!"—and then Idaho— "Everything out here in the West seems so BIG! Mom said it would be. Just look at those mountains over there. They're like Mount Everest or something." She paused only long enough to take a big breath. "Did I tell you about the time I skateboarded down Gwynn Island Hill over by Herrington Lake? It was a big hill, too . . . for Kentucky, anyway. I was moving as fast as a fly before the swatter by the time I reached the bottom of that thing."

Tucker let out a sigh. *It is time to prepare for the hunt.*

"Say, Tucker, can you belch whenever you want to?" Livi asked cheerfully.

Duane Renfro laughed again. "Where did you get your sense of humor, Livi? It couldn't have been from your m——"

He stopped short, then tapped his fingers on the steering wheel and joined Tucker looking out over the forested landscape of Northern Idaho.

Livi passed her wide smile back and forth across the front seat. "I can belch on command. Mom acts like she doesn't like it. She's funny. She tries to hide her smile. But if someone says, 'Belch,' I'll do it."

Tucker noticed a deer standing on the edge of a meadow, mostly hidden in the afternoon shadows. *My bow is almost ready, handcrafted from the limb of a birch tree.*

Duane Renfro turned his car off the main highway onto a gravel county road. A plume of dust kicked up as he accelerated across a set of railroad tracks and moved up a hill. A partially finished log house sat beside a mobile home on one side of the road. Farther up was a junkyard with a house in the middle—old car parts, discarded window frames, rusty buckets, and gray lumber piled around a shack covered with black roofing paper instead of siding.

"Tamarack Road," Duane Renfro said as much to himself as Livi. "Almost home."

Livi sat back in her seat. "I can't believe I'm here," she said with a giggle. "The wild West! Just like Mom said! I've got a letter already written to send her. I wrote it on the plane. She mailed one to me before I even left Kentucky. Is it here yet?"

Duane nodded yes. "It came Saturday."

The station wagon slowed and pulled into a narrow driveway. Duane turned off the ignition and pointed toward a small one-story house with a tin roof and wood siding stained dark brown. To the side was a makeshift turkey coop and pen, in back of that a garage. A shaggy, cinnamon-colored dog was curled on the porch, asleep. "I know it's not as nice as what you're used to, Livi," Duane said, "but it sure is great to have you at our house."

Livi beamed up at him from the backseat. "I'm as pleased as fruit punch, too, Dad." Then with a wild lunge forward, she pointed to the banged-up Volkswagen parked beside the Renfro garage. "Slug Bug!" she yelled, and punched both her brother and her father playfully on the arm.

# 3

"And this is where you'll sleep," Duane Renfro was saying to Livi. Tucker stopped for a moment and listened to the voices of his father and sister in the back of the house. He then quietly pulled the door closed behind him and stepped out onto the porch.

The dog, Maggie, rose from her regular spot near the steps and yawned. "What Dad means is that Livi will be sleeping in *my* room," Tucker muttered to her. His voice came out even more sour as he mimicked the earlier conversation between him and his father: "It will just be for a while, Tucker. It's not that much to do for your own sister, is it?"

Tucker jumped down from the porch steps. He looked back at the house, then at Maggie. She had

13

returned to her spot, curled on the doormat, chin resting on her paws. "Stay," Tucker said, in case she decided to follow him. He turned and slipped quickly out the driveway, and toward the woods on the other side of Tamarack Road.

The red flag was up on the mailbox. Tucker stopped and looked at it. Olivia had run there right from the car and put in the letter to Kentucky. "There!" she had beamed at Tucker and Duane, who were still standing in the driveway with her suitcases in hand. "A letter written is a letter received. Mom writes such good letters. I can't wait to see what she wrote me before I left, knowing I'd open it on my first day in Idaho! She'll write every day! It's almost like she's here!" She reached over and gently stroked the mailbox the same way you would a sleeping cat. "I just *love* mailboxes, don't you?"

Tucker had answered with only a steady stare, the same he now gave the mailbox. He reached up and touched the red flag, then let his hand move slowly down. He traced the curl of the aluminum handle with a fingertip, then gripped it. With a gentle tug, he opened the door.

The letter lay faceup. Tucker could clearly see the address: Ms. Kathy Hayden, 1169 Crosshill Road, Lexington, Kentucky 40502. The carefully printed words and numbers seemed to jump off the white envelope. The address was one he knew by heart. It was also one he seldom heard from or wrote to. He shut the mailbox door, then turned and hopped the ditch beside the county road.

When he reached the woods, Tucker broke quickly into a run. Jumping logs and cutting around stumps, he wove through the trees and onto a narrow, downward-sloping path.

At the bottom of a hill, Tucker stopped and rested beside a dry creek bed. He was breathing heavily. Sweat had soaked through his shirt. The cloth fell cool against his skin. He wiped his forehead. *I am about to enter the place of The Tribe. A brave should do so only with a clear mind.* He calmed his breathing and inspected the creek bed. Large rocks that were stepping-stones in wetter times sat in the middle of cracked mud. He stepped on them anyway as he crossed.

On the other side of the creek bed, Tucker looked quickly over his shoulder, then knelt and crawled through a tunnel-like opening in a thicket of low willows. *Here I can prepare for my first hunt.*

The tunnel curled around a large cedar tree, then opened up to a small clearing. Tucker stood and crossed the clearing, stopping only for a moment at a fire pit circled with stones to set up a log seat that had fallen over. He then walked to a small tipi made from lashed branches covered with old wool blankets.

Tucker knelt and crawled inside. *I must write all*

*important events in the journal.* In the back of the tipi was another old blanket spread out on the ground. Tucker folded it back. A piece of plywood lay beneath. He brushed off the dirt and pushed the plywood to one side to reveal a round coffee can neatly sunk into a hole dug in the ground. He pulled it out and pried off the plastic lid. A small spiral notebook was curled inside. *It's The Tribe's record book, almost three years now.* Pulling the notebook out of the can, Tucker gently uncurled it and looked at the cover. It was decorated with tiny pictures of tipis, Indian hunters on horseback, buffalo, spears, bows and arrows, and shields. In the center was an Indian chief sitting in front of a stretched buffalo hide, paintbrush in hand. WINTER COUNT: A HISTORY OF THE TRIBE was printed neatly in large black letters on the hide. *Just like the Indians used the buffalo skins to record important events.*

Tucker scooted over to the better light of the tipi doorway and opened the notebook. He turned each page slowly, scanning dated entries here and there as he went: *July 13, Season of the Drought: Forest fires are out of control in Montana and in Eastern Washington. We're expecting trouble in North Idaho, too. No fires in the fire pit. October 31, Season of Early Snows: Snowshoe hares haven't turned all white yet. Easy to see. April 1, Season of Mud: Joe Allen and I had a mud ball fight by the creek this afternoon. He yelled "Geronimo!" My mud ball went right into his open mouth.* Tucker laughed softly, then read on. *January 23, Midwinter Thaw: Where is all the snow? May 18, Season of Flowers: I found just the right piece of birchwood for my bow, and some good ones for my arrows, too! Dad says he'll help me with it and take me on my first hunt.*

Tucker continued reading until he came to blank pages. He reached back and picked up a ball-point pen from the coffee can and dated his entry: *September 5 (Labor Day) . . .* He hesitated for a moment, then started to write again. . . . *Season of Olivia's Arriv*——

A sound from across the dry creek bed stopped him. It was the sharp snap of a twig breaking underfoot.

In one quick motion, Tucker set the journal down and rose. Grabbing a long, straight stick with an old sock bunched and tied around the tip from beside the tipi, he crouched low and slipped noiselessly into the willow thicket.

Seconds later a boy's freckled face peered from the tunnel entrance and around the big cedar, eyes wide in anticipation. "Rats!" the boy whispered to himself when he saw no one. He reached up and picked a piece of tree bark from his curly red hair.

The boy rose into a crouched position and slowly entered the clearing, eyes moving quickly from side to side, scanning the surrounding brush. He carried a sock-tipped spear just like Tucker's in his left hand, held as if ready to throw. He knelt by the fire pit and put his hand in the ashes. They were cold. He wrinkled his nose and scanned the willow thicket again. "Guess he's not here," the boy said, then relaxed his body and stood. He set down his spear, reached into his pocket, and pulled out a piece of chewing gum, unwrapped it, then popped it into his mouth.

"YAH!" Tucker sprang up from the brush and threw his spear. The blunted sock tip hit the boy square in the chest as he turned in surprise. His gum fell out of his mouth onto the ground.

"OW! Tucker, don't throw so hard."

"Gotcha, Joe Allen," Tucker said proudly, walking over to the fire pit. "I gotcha fair and square. Pretty good, huh?"

Joe Allen Vickstrom leaned over and picked up his gum. Tiny bits of dirt and sticks clung to it. He tried to pick them off, then shrugged and put the gum back in his mouth. "Yeah, it was a good shot," he said. "But you really don't have to throw so hard. What if you had hit me in the face?"

Tucker picked up his spear, then Joe Allen's. He leaned them both against the cedar tree. "I wouldn't," he said matter-of-factly, then walked over to the tipi.

Joe Allen rubbed his chest where the spear had hit him. He followed Tucker across the clearing. "What're you writing in Winter Count?" he asked when he saw the open spiral notebook.

Tucker sat down and quickly closed it. "Nothing," he said with a hint of anger in his voice.

Disbelief showed plainly on Joe Allen's face. "Hey, Winter Count is *our* book. You said we are brothers bound in blood, warriors of The Tribe, just like the Indians that used to live around here. What are you writing?"

Tucker looked down at the notebook, then let out a sigh. "All right. I came here to write about preparing for our first deer hunt. But then . . . well, I found myself writing about my sister instead."

Joe Allen's red eyebrows shot up in surprise. "Sister? You never told me you had a sister!"

Tucker shrugged. "I never felt like I did. She's been living in Kentucky with my mom all this time. My parents have suddenly agreed that I should get to know Olivia."

Joe Allen wrinkled his nose in disgust. "Olivia?"

"Yep, that's her name."

"Bad news," Joe Allen said, shaking his head. "I know all about sisters. I've got three of them. Is she younger or older?"

"Younger."

"Eeeee!" Joe Allen exclaimed, clutching at his heart as if pierced by an arrow. "That's the worst kind. And with a name like Olivia?"

Tucker nodded. "She's at the house right now. Dad gave her *my* room to sleep in. I had to clear out all of my personal stuff. He moved the junk in the big hall closet out to the garage, then turned the hall closet into my bedroom."

Joe Allen shook his head. "And I'll bet your dad made it sound like a great thing to do for your sister, huh? Giving up your own room. Adults always say that kind of stuff."

Tucker nodded. "And get this—she's going to go to school here until Thanksgiving!"

Joe Allen's eyebrows shot up again. "Oooo! More bad news; enough to turn your mind to stumps."

The clearing lapsed quiet for a moment. Joe Allen took the gum from his mouth and inspected it for signs of dirt. Tucker reached into his pocket and pulled out the carved Indian chief's head. He ran his fingers over the smooth wood, then placed the small carving back in his pocket. Opening the notebook again, he read the beginning of his new entry: *September 5 (Labor Day): Season of Olivia's Arriv——*.

Tucker picked up the pen. *A clear mind.* He

crossed out Olivia's name and the rest of the entry with big Xs. Then he began again: *September 5 (Labor Day): Season of the Hunt—I have stalked the sleeping bear. With a clear mind I am ready to prepare for the hunt.*

# 4

"Can I be excused?" Tucker asked his father from across the kitchen table.

Duane Renfro glanced over at Livi, who was busily picking the black olives off her piece of pizza and stacking them up on the side of her plate. She stopped what she was doing and smiled at him—the big, ear-to-ear grin she had been throwing around the table all through the meal. He returned her smile, then looked back to his son. "What's the hurry, Tucker?"

Tucker shrugged. "I just thought I'd get things ready for the start of school tomorrow: notebooks, pencils, erasers, things like that."

Duane Renfro wiped his mouth with his napkin,

then took a sip of his coffee. "This has been a very quiet meal. I thought we could all sit and talk for a while."

Livi looked up again from her pile of black olives. "Yeah, Tucker, I was wondering if you could tell me about Indians," she said. "Dad says you know a lot about them. Do they still live around here?"

Tucker scooted his chair back and stood up. His hand slid into his pocket and held the Indian chief carving. *The ways of The Tribe are to always be kept secret.* "I really have a lot to do," he said. "Sixth grade, you know. I want to get off to a good sta—"

"I thought that maybe we could play some Monopoly, too," Duane cut in, "or take turns challenging each other at chess. Livi tells me she plays."

Tucker let the carving slip out of his hand, back to the bottom of his pants pocket. "Dad, can I *please* be excused?" he asked again.

Duane Renfro set his coffee cup down and looked squarely at his son. "It's your turn to do the dishes," he said firmly.

Despite the stern tone of his father's voice, Tucker started to protest. "But, Dad—"

"I'll do them," Livi cut in.

Tucker and Duane both looked at her in surprise.

She stood up and smiled. "I don't mind, really. We have a dishwasher at home. Mom just pops the dirty dishes in and turns it on. She says that gives us more time together in the evening."

Duane pointed to Tucker and started to speak. Livi quickly pulled the letter from Kentucky out of her pocket and held it up. "Mom and I have a great time in the evenings. We take turns reading out loud to each other, kind of acting out the parts. Or we play chess, or watch football games. We both like the Cincinnati Bengals. But anyway, I never get to wash the dishes. It'd be fun to play with the bubbles." She picked up the rest of her piece of pizza and crammed it into her mouth. "I'm finished, see?" she said through the wad of dough, then began to clear the table. "You go get ready for school, Tucker. We can talk or play games later."

"Thanks," Tucker said in a near whisper. Without looking at his father, he quickly turned and went to the old closet that was now his new room. He pulled the chain to turn on the bare light bulb, then shut the door behind him.

Tucker took a long, blanket-wrapped bundle from behind a roll of old carpet and placed it gently on the mattress his father had laid out for him on the closet floor. He untied the leather thongs and set them to one side. The bundle unrolled most of the way by itself. Tucker finished by spreading the corners flat. He looked at the contents. A bow—still unstrung—and three arrows now lay in the center of his bed.

Tucker picked up the bow and ran his fingers over the smooth birchwood. *The hunter's bow must become like a part of his own body if he is to use it well.* Hours of sanding had left no bumps or splintered ends anywhere on the bow's length. The natural curve he had found in that particular birch tree limb by the creek last spring still held true from tip to tip. The notches for the bowstring lined up perfectly on both ends. The grip fit easily in his palm. *Dad hasn't had much time to help me like he said he would. But it's better that I've done the work myself anyway. By making the bow the hunter knows it as well as he knows his own hands.* All that he still had to do was rub the wood with oil to keep it from drying out and getting brittle.

Carefully placing the bow on the blanket, Tucker picked up each of the three arrows in turn and sighted down their length. *Each shaft has to be as straight as I want it to fly, each fire-hardened tip as sharp as chipped stone, each feather as true as a bird's wing.* He checked the tightness of the fishing line he had used to bind the split feathers to the shaft. "Almost done," he said, with a smile. "Just in time. Deer season opens in less than two weeks."

Tucker twirled one of the arrows in his palm. *I will kill the deer with one shot to the—*

A knock came on his bedroom door. Livi's voice bounced merrily as she spoke. "Dad said he'd finish the dishes, Tucker. He's just scrubbing away and listening to some old jazz tapes he's got. He said I should come spend some time with you. Great idea, huh? Can I come in?"

Tucker didn't hesitate in answering. "No."

There was a moment of silence. Tucker could see the shadow of Livi's feet under the door. She giggled. There was a rustling sound, then scratching. Seconds later a slip of paper was pushed under the door into the room. *I DON'T BITE,* it said in big letters.

Tucker wrapped the bow and arrows in the blanket again and tied it with the leather thongs. He ignored Livi's note, but listened intently. She waited for a minute or two, then walked quickly down the hall to his old room and returned. Another note was pushed under the door. This one had a penny taped to it. ENTRANCE FEE—1 PENNY was printed above the coin.

Tucker walked over and pushed both notes back under. Livi ran down the hall. A few seconds later she was back. More scratching could be heard, then lots of tearing sounds. Tucker got down on his belly and tried to look under the door. Bits of paper were falling onto the hall floor around Livi's feet. Her hands came into view and picked them up. There was a moment of silence. Then she got down on her hands and knees. Tucker pushed himself back as the open end of an envelope slowly appeared under the door. He craned his neck forward to see what she had written this time. A big puff of air hit him square in the face. She had blown into the other side of the envelope. Bits of paper flew into his eyes and even his mouth.

"Yuck!" he yelled.

"Oh, no!" Livi's voice came from out in the hall. She jumped up and pushed on the door. It flew partway open, hitting Tucker right in the middle of his forehead. He rolled away with a groan, thumping the back of his head on the wall.

The closet door slowly opened the rest of the way. Livi's face appeared, eyes wide. "Tucker, I'm sorry. I didn't know you were—" She stopped and bowed her head as he glared up at her.

Tucker stood.

"Maybe we could talk about Indians," she said in a tiny voice.

Tucker didn't move.

"And buffalo. Do you ever see buffalo in your backyard?"

Tucker's only answer was to take a deep breath and clinch his fists. Livi backed slowly out of the closet, turned, and walked down the hall. The sounds of Duane Renfro's old jazz tape filtered back from the front of the house, filling the space between them. Livi quietly shut her bedroom door. Tucker barricaded his own.

# 5

The buck raised his head and sniffed the early morning air of September 6 for danger, antlers spread out above him like a white-tipped crown. Ears rotated back and forth, keen for any unusual sound. He stomped the ground nervously with a front hoof.

Tucker couldn't hold his breath any longer. He let the stale air out of his lungs as slowly as he could. *I have to keep my breath very shallow so it doesn't show in this cold air.* He had left the house without a jacket to climb the birch tree and watch for deer. Now his fingers were numb in the cold and damp, and a knot on the tree trunk was digging into his back. Still, he didn't move a muscle. *I've seen this buck here every morning for a week. I'm close enough for a shot. I will become a hunter.*

29

The buck lowered his head and again pulled at the last of the summer clover on the edge of the Renfros' small meadow. Tucker shifted his weight on the tree limb. The buck's head shot up. Tucker froze.

A screen door slammed. Tucker slowly moved his eyes from the deer until he could see his house up by the road. His father, feed bucket in hand, was headed for the turkey pen. Livi bounced along beside him like a puppy following its master. Their voices drifted into the woods, muffled by the distance and early morning fog. Light laughter from Livi was the only clear sound that reached Tucker's ears. He tightened his fists. *The Tribe is for members only! Outsiders will always stay just that—outside!*

Without thinking, Tucker reached up and felt the knot on his forehead from where the closet door had hit him. The buck caught the movement of Tucker's hand out of the corner of his eye. In a flash of brown and white he bounded into the woods and disappeared.

Tucker watched him go, then turned back to the house. "Good morning, *Olivia*," he said angrily, then climbed down from among the yellowing leaves of the birch tree and headed home.

An hour later, Tucker walked out the kitchen door and headed for the bus stop, school notebook in hand. His father's voice caught him halfway down the driveway.

"Hey, Tucker, did I tell you I have a job interview today?"

Tucker turned. Duane Renfro stood on the porch steps dressed in a white shirt, slacks, tie, and a sport coat. Tucker's face lit up. "Wow, Dad! I was wondering why you were taking so long getting dressed. What's the job?"

Duane straightened his tie a bit. He reached down and patted Maggie on the head. She stood beside him, wagging her tail as if his getting dressed up excited her, too. "It's not much, just . . . well, actually it could be a real break for me. It's with the school district."

The smile on Tucker's face grew even larger. "You're going to go back to teaching?" He was up on the porch beside his father before he finished the question. "I thought you didn't like all the hassles—"

Duane Renfro raised his hand like a cop at an intersection. "It's only a tutoring position. There's a kid who got hurt over the summer in a bicycle accident and is in a big cast and can't come to school."

Tucker couldn't stop smiling. "Yeah, but it's a *job*. It's been so long since you've tried . . . since you've had a chance."

"It would only be temporary and part-time,"

Duane said, "but it might get my foot in the door for a better position later." He rubbed his chin and smiled. "I guess the chance is worth a shave, anyway."

Livi opened the door and stepped out onto the porch. She wore a red-checked dress and shiny black shoes and carried a satchel under her arm. "Well, what do you think?" she asked with a big smile. "I guess I look like I'm ready to waltz with the king, huh?"

Duane laughed and motioned toward his tie. "Then I must be ready to waltz with the queen."

Livi walked over and stood beside her father. Tucker turned and stepped down from the porch.

"Mom says the clothes make the woman," Livi said to Duane. "She made me promise to dress up on the first day of school. She said I could wear my T-shirt with the drawing of the solar system on the front and my high-top leopard-spot sneakers the second day. She must have talked to you about first impressions, too."

Duane shifted uneasily, then busied himself adjusting his tie. Tucker looked down at his own clothes—jeans, a plaid shirt, and dirty basketball shoes. "Bus will be here soon," he said.

Livi turned her large brown eyes on Tucker. They sparkled with excitement. "I feel just deliverous!" she said, prancing down the steps toward him.

Duane looked up and laughed. "I think you mean delirious," he said. "As good as you can imagine, huh? Remember, though, this is a country school, not what you're used to in Lexington, Kentucky."

"Whatever," Livi said, "I'm ready! Let's go, brother!"

Tucker looked at her as if she had asked him to go walk off the edge of Chimney Rock. He reached up and touched the bump on his forehead. There was a moment of silence.

Duane finally broke it. "You go on, Livi. The bus will stop at the end of the driveway. I want to talk with Tucker for a minute."

Livi looked up at her father. "Good luck with the job interview, Dad." She beamed. "You can do it, I know you can." She gave Maggie a pat on the head, then bounced off toward Tamarack Road.

Duane waited until Livi was out of earshot before he spoke. "You've been mighty hard on your sister, Tucker." It was the same firm voice of the night before—the one that Duane used only when he was upset. Tucker pushed at the gravel in the driveway with his foot. He kept his eyes down.

"Why won't you give her a chance?" Duane asked, eyes searching.

Tucker kept pushing the gravel with his foot, eyes down.

"She just wants to get to know you."

*She is an outsider. Things were fine before she came.*

"She is your sister," Duane reminded him.

Tucker kicked at the gravel. His words spilled out angrily: "Your daughter, you mean! I don't remember my sister!"

Duane Renfro's reaction came in quick, firm movements. But by the time he was off the porch and had laid his hand on Tucker's shoulder, the touch was soft and pleading. Tucker looked up into eyes that showed pain.

"I'm sorry that you don't know Olivia," Duane said. He looked out at the bus stop. Livi waved cheerfully. He waved back, trying to send her a long-distance smile. "But she is here because she *wants* to change that," he said, looking back down at Tucker. "She told me this morning that your mother has been talking about working at getting us all back together again. She said your mother still loves me, even after all of these years apart. I don't know if that's true, but I do know I'm going to go into that job interview today and really try this time, not look for reasons to say no. Livi said she is going to write your mother every day, tell her what a great family we could be. I saw her addressing another envelope after breakfast. Maybe my trying to do something with my life will make a difference to all of us. Maybe you could help, too, huh?"

Tucker reached into his pocket and felt the carved Indian chief. *Only for members of The Tribe.*

"Tucker?" Duane's voice came as a plea from above him. "Can you please at least *try* to give Livi a chance? If not for her, then for me?"

The carved Indian chief rolled smoothly around in Tucker's hand. He ran his fingers over the carved feathers of the war bonnet, down onto the sharp lines of the face. "I'll try, Dad," he said, "I'll try."

# 6

Joe Allen looked around him in the crowded school bus to see if anybody was watching, snuck his brown lunch sack up close to his face, and peered inside. "Ah, tuna fish," he whispered to Tucker.

Tucker leaned over in the school bus seat and looked into Joe Allen's lunch sack. A tuna fish sandwich lay in the bottom. A big red apple had squashed it into the shape of a bowl.

"Looks damaged," Tucker said with a smirk.

Joe Allen's red eyebrows shot up in fake alarm. "Damaged?" he asked in a high, squeaky voice. "How *dare* you talk about my sandwich like that?"

Tucker gave him a sidelong glance. "Oh, did I say damaged? I'm sorry. I meant to say *dangerous*. It looks *dangerous*, don't you think?"

Joe Allen quickly closed his lunch sack and hit Tucker on the shoulder with it.

Tucker broke into a big grin. "Help!" he yelled just quiet enough not to be heard by the bus driver. "I'm being attacked by a tuna fish sandwich. I told you it was dangerous." He picked up his own sack to fight back. Livi's smiling face appeared over the back of the bus seat just as he was about to swing at Joe Allen's head. He stopped in an instant. *I promised Dad I'd try to be nice.*

"Hi," he said, his voice forced.

"Why, howdy-ho to you, too, Tucker," Livi said, her smile expanding from ear to ear. "You boys starting off the school year with a little bus ruckus?"

Joe Allen twisted around in his seat to get a better look.

"You must be Joe Allen Vickstrom," Livi said.

Joe Allen looked over at Tucker. "How did she know that?"

*I promised Dad I'd try to be nice. When a member of The Tribe makes a promise, he is honor-bound to keep that promise no matter—*

"I've got ears the size of rhinoceros wings, that's how," Livi said, turning her head and pointing at one ear with her finger. "You'd be amazed at what I know and can do."

Joe Allen's red eyebrows rose. He scrunched up his nose. "Your ears look normal to me. You must be Olivia, huh?"

She leaned a bit closer. "Livi. And I can burp on command."

Joe Allen laughed. He looked at Tucker.

Tucker shrugged. *Try to be nice.*

Joe Allen looked back at Livi. "Oh, yeah?"

She nodded and opened her mouth in the shape of an O. "I keep my mouth ready to burp. See?"

Joe Allen nodded. "So do it, then."

A loud burp rolled out of Livi's open mouth. Two high-school girls across the bus aisle stopped talking and looked over.

Livi smiled at them as if her burping were a private joke.

Joe Allen nudged Tucker with his elbow. "You didn't tell me your sister was so talented."

Tucker shrugged again. *I am honor-bound to keep my promise to Dad.*

Turning all the way around in his seat, Joe Allen faced Livi, who still sat with her mouth in the shape of an O. "Listen to this," he said, and let out an even louder burp.

One of the high-school girls leaned over and tapped Joe Allen on the shoulder. "That's disgusting," she said down her nose at him. He looked back at Livi with a twinkle in his eye. "That girl says that we're disgusting, Olivia."

Tucker turned away from Joe Allen and his sister and looked out the bus window. *He likes her! Joe Allen is a member of The Tribe and he likes her! I can't believe it.* Mr. Eldridge's pond came into view as the bus rounded a corner. *But I am a warrior of The Tribe. I will keep my promise, no matter how I feel.* A flock of Canadian geese paddled on the still water of the pond. Tucker put his finger on the bus window glass and counted. There were fourteen.

Livi leaned close to Joe Allen's ear. A very small burp came out of her O-shaped mouth. "Call me Livi, not Olivia," she said. "And that burp was only half as loud, so I guess it was only half as disgusting, right?"

Joe Allen laughed, rubbing his hands together. Then he burped softly—twice.

Livi's mouth went immediately into the shape of an O again. She burped three times in a row, quickly drawing in her throat muscles to catch air each time.

Four burps came back at her from Joe Allen. His ears started to turn red.

Livi responded with six, then took a deep breath and did three more without pausing for additional air.

Joe Allen elbowed Tucker. "Are you counting?"

A doe and her spotted fawn crossed the road in front of the bus and jumped a fence. Tucker shrugged off Joe Allen's question and kept his eyes glued to the window.

"She did *nine!*" Joe Allen exclaimed. "But listen to this!" A string of burps rocketed out of his mouth, each getting louder as they came.

The high-school girls looked at each other. "Disgusting," they said at the same time, then rolled their eyes and laughed.

"Yep!" Joe Allen agreed with a burp and a smile.

"A regular bus ruckus!" Livi whooped. "How *disgusting!*"

Tucker looked at Joe Allen, Olivia, then back out the school bus window. "Yeah, it's disgusting all right," he whispered to the glass.

# 7

Tucker dropped to his belly and rested the side of his face on the forest floor. He squinted, closing one eye and then the other, staring hard at a spot only inches away. Gently, he reached out and ran his fingers over it—a slight depression on a patch of bare soil. A smile spread across his mouth. *That's it! That's the next track. I thought I'd lost that buck's trail in all of those leaves, but that's his next footprint right there!*

Careful not to disturb even one leaf or twig, Tucker crept forward, feeling ahead with his fingers, scanning with his eyes. *The next one should be right . . . there!* He put his finger down in another track, this one in softer soil. *I can feel the*

41

*two points of the split hoof!* He let his fingers roam. *And there's the front hoof! It's right over from the back print, just like Dad showed me last spring. So the next set should be* . . . He reached forward again.

"Yahoo!" Tucker shouted joyfully into the trees as he found the next print. "I'm tracking a deer! I, Tucker J. Renfro, am tracking a real live deer through the woods!" *I will be a hunter for The Tribe.*

He moved forward again, and again, and again, placing his fingers into the small rounded tracks— sets of two, front and rear, diagonally laid in a zigzag pattern. *This is easy!* Tucker stood and looked through the trees. *There's the trail! It goes right around the meadow and our house, just like a freeway bypass for deer! How many times have I crossed it and not noticed?*

Tucker moved quickly, following the path. It bordered the meadow, then dropped down into a shallow gully and along the barbed-wire fence that marked the family property line. He could plainly see a worn spot in the weeds on the other side where the deer had jumped over. There were even a few tufts of deer hair caught in one of the barbs on the top strand. The trail then went up the gully toward Tamarack Road. Tucker smiled. *Now I know why I see so many deer crossing the road right here.*

*Next thing you know, they'll be putting in a cross-walk like at school, right here by my house!*

His house. The thought of it pushed the smile from Tucker's face in an instant. He peered over the edge of the gully, through the trees. Only parts of the brown siding were visible, the afternoon sun glaring off the tin roof here and there, the garage in back, the turkey pen to the side. But he could see all of Olivia. She sat on the porch. She'd been there over an hour now, bent over her notebook—writing. *Probably a letter to Kentucky. She got another one today from Mom. Held it out for me to read. "Mom asked about you, Tucker," she said. "She wanted to know how you are doing." I saw Mom's handwriting on the envelope—so perfect, just like on the ones I keep in my sock drawer. Mom writes as pretty as she looks in the picture she sent two years ago.*

Tucker squinted, as if doing so would give him telescopic vision, allowing him to read what Olivia was writing. *I'll bet she's not telling Mom how I'm doing. She doesn't even know how I'm doing. She's probably telling her how Dad didn't get the job with the school district. How he was sitting on the porch with a bottle of whiskey when we got home from school. She's probably writing all about how he was still dressed in the sport coat, white shirt, and tie he had worn to the job interview. How he stumbled when he stood and walked out to meet us. How he said he didn't want that tutoring job anyway, he'd just get another odd job to keep us going. Then how he almost fell down.*

*Dad gets drunk sometimes. So what? He's just too smart for most jobs. He's got two college degrees. He could be a professor if he wanted to. And he apologized to us for being drunk, didn't he? He poured the rest of the bottle out and went inside, didn't he? He said he'd try again somewhere else tomorrow. He will if he said he will. I know it.*

Olivia looked up as if thinking what to write next, then bent over her paper again.

*Why does she have to get Dad's hopes up? Why does she have to write Mom every day? Mom was never satisfied with the way he was. She's probably still perfect, just like her handwriting. He's my dad. That's enough for me. Don't write about me, or Dad, or anything, Olivia! We are better off on our own.*

Olivia continued to write, Tucker to watch.

*Better off without you here, that's for sure. It seems like every time I turn around you're grinning up at me like I should pet you or something, like you can make everything perfect just by smiling at it. You smiled at Dad that way today and then helped him inside and fixed him some coffee. I was going to do that. What do you think you're doing?*

*Taking over? And MY friend Joe Allen actually likes you because you can burp a bunch of times in a row. Why do you have to write all of those letters? Why do you have to be here?*

Tucker looked away from his house, back at the deer tracks. *Well, this is my deer, Olivia. MY deer, not yours. I can track him. I can shoot him with my bow and arrow—one shot to the chest. Dad said he'll help me, and he will. I WILL be a hunter for The Tribe.*

He left then, crossing the fence, the county road, and walking into the woods. Following the tracks of the deer, Tucker's eyes not once lifted from the ground until his house was completely out of sight.

# 8

Tucker crept out of the brush, soft-tipped spear in hand. Joe Allen was sitting in the doorway of the tipi, writing furiously in Winter Count. Tucker moved forward. *Joe Allen deserves to get speared— both for being easy to sneak up on, and for being so friendly to Olivia.* He raised the spear to throw.

"Twenty-eight times, Tucker!" Joe Allen blurted out without looking up.

Tucker frowned and lowered his spear. "You heard me coming. How did you hear me? I was being quiet."

Joe Allen looked up, a scowl on his freckled face. "Twenty-eight times that sister of yours burped without stopping! I almost passed out from lack of

46

oxygen at number nineteen. How am I ever going to play the clarinet if a fourth-grade girl can beat me in a burping contest?"

A smile crept onto Tucker's face. *Good! Joe Allen found out fast what a pain Olivia can be.* He leaned his spear against the big cedar. "Since when are you interested in playing the clarinet?"

Joe Allen's frown curled up into a smile. "Since Jessica Wagner is going to play clarinet in the sixth-grade band."

Tucker sat down. "What are you talking about?"

The smile on Joe Allen's face widened. He put Winter Count down. "Tucker, haven't you noticed how good-looking Jessica Wagner got over the summer? It's like she ate beauty pills or something. Now she's smart *and* pretty." The grin faded. "But she's in Mr. Hanna's room. I'll never get to sit by her unless I play the clarinet in the band."

Tucker picked up Winter Count. "Is that what you were writing about? Clarinets and Jessica Wagner?"

The scowl pushed back onto Joe Allen's face again. "No, I was writing about that sister of yours."

Tucker stiffened. *Winter Count is the journal of The Tribe. Olivia is NOT part of The Tribe. I crossed her out. Can't he see that?*

"Twenty-eight burps!" Joe Allen repeated. "Can

you believe it? To get beat by a fourth-grade girl is a terrible thing."

Tucker let his shoulders drop. *At least Joe Allen doesn't think Olivia is so great anymore.* "Just ignore her," he said. "That's what I do."

Joe Allen wasn't through. "And now she says we should have a ruler-balancing contest—you know, on the end of your finger. I'll bet I have fingers that don't work any better than my burps!"

Tucker opened Winter Count and looked at Joe Allen's entry. It was so scrawled he couldn't read it. "Just ignore my sister," he said. "We should be getting ready for the hunt. Deer season opens just one week from this coming Saturday. We have to finish our bows and the arrows, test them, and then practice a lot, too."

"A girl!" Joe Allen said, shaking his head. "If I can't beat a *girl*, I'll never be able to play the clarinet. Then I'll never be able to sit next to Jessica Wagner."

Tucker went on: "I was reading last night about how some of the Indian tribes prepared for important events. Sometimes the braves stayed in skin huts filled with steam to purify themselves."

Joe Allen shrugged, then wrinkled his nose. "Hey, Tucker, did I show you my dirty-word list?"

"And a tribe called the Mandans had a ritual for becoming a brave," Tucker said. "They stuck hooks through the muscles on their chests and got strung up on ropes till the hooks tore out. It was a test of bravery, or worthiness, I guess. Can you believe they did that? Wow!"

Joe Allen pulled a piece of paper from the back pocket of his jeans and unfolded it. "I've got twenty-one, no . . . twenty-three dirty words on my list. Want to hear them?"

Tucker kept right on talking. "This book I was reading even had drawings done by the first white man ever to see the Mandan ritual," he said. "His name was George Catlin."

"Number sixteen is one of my favorite dirty words of all time," Joe Allen continued. "You want to hear number sixteen?"

"That must have been something," Tucker mused, "to be the first white man to see those braves hanging from their hooks in their chests."

Joe Allen held his list up in front of Tucker's face. "Which dirty word do you like best?"

Tucker ignored the paper, looking up instead at the bright blue September sky. "We should do something to prove our worthiness, too. We would be known for our bravery throughout The Tribe. I'd be called Deer Tracker. Joe Allen, you'd be called—"

"C'mon, pick one," Joe Allen insisted.

"What?" Tucker turned toward Joe Allen as he spoke.

"Which dirty word on my list do you like best?"

Tucker's face went red. "We're talking about getting ready for the hunt, not your dirty-word list!"

Joe Allen shook the paper in front of Tucker's face. "You've got to have a favorite. Which one?"

Anger rose in Tucker's voice. "This is the place of The Tribe, not the bathroom at school. We're supposed to keep a clear mind when we come here, remember? Deer season starts two weeks from this coming Saturday. We've got to get ready!"

Joe Allen wouldn't quit. "Timothy Potts gave me a great one. Look at number twenty on my list."

"Joe Allen!" Tucker pushed the paper away. Joe Allen narrowed his eyes and pushed it back. A quick round of push and shove erupted. Winter Count fell to the dirt.

"Now look what you've done!" Tucker yelled, jumping up.

Joe Allen's eyes went wide. "ME?" he shouted, getting quickly to his feet.

Tucker picked up the journal and brushed it off. "Yes, YOU! You don't care about the hunt. You don't care about The Tribe. All you're interested in is clarinets, Jessica Wagner, burps, and dirty words!"

Joe Allen quickly looked down and scanned the list that was still in his hand. "Snollygoster!" he yelled into Tucker's face.

Tucker took a step forward. "What did you call me?"

"Snollygoster," Joe Allen repeated defiantly. "I called you a snollygoster."

Tucker balled up his fists and raised them. Joe Allen did the same. Both looked angrily into each other's eyes. There was a moment of silence in the clearing. Each waited for the other to take the first swing.

"And just what is a snollygoster?" Tucker finally asked.

Joe Allen's fists lowered a bit. He wrinkled his nose. "I don't know."

The giggle that came out of Tucker's mouth escaped on its own. He tried to continue looking angry, but a smile fought its way onto his lips. "You don't know what the word means?"

Joe Allen shrugged. "Ask Timothy Potts. He gave it to me. He said it was a great dirty word."

They both smiled at the same time.

"Timothy Potts?" Tucker said. "You can't believe anything that he says. He probably just saw the word somewhere in the dictionary. Snollygoster is probably just the name of some African animal or something."

Joe Allen snickered. "Or an auto part."

"Or Jessica Wagner's middle name," Tucker added with a laugh. "Jessica *Snollygoster* Wagner."

Joe Allen's fists went back up, but this time they were accompanied by a smile. Tucker's did also.

"Snollygoster!" Joe Allen yelled.

"Snollygoster to you, too!" Tucker came right back at him.

They play-boxed around the clearing, jabbing and blocking, laughing and yelling at each other, full of the last little bit of summer.

# 9

"Tucker, I've got a small job over at the Eldridges today helping them roof their new barn," Duane Renfro said from across the kitchen table.

Tucker looked up from his Saturday breakfast. The circles under his father's eyes seemed especially dark in the overhead kitchen light. Duane had been up almost all night again, searching newspaper want ads for job openings, copying down phone numbers, writing letters, then writing them over and over again.

Duane ran his hand over the stubble of his beard, then took another sip of coffee. "I want you to keep Livi company today—"

"Aw, Dad!" Tucker was out of his chair in an

53

instant. He moved quickly around to where his father sat. "I've got plans with Joe Allen. And Olivia's such a . . ." He hesitated. "Well, I've got plans."

The hurt came quickly into his father's eyes, just as Tucker had seen it every day that week when Olivia sealed an envelope and took a Kentucky-bound letter out to the mailbox. And especially last night when the phone call came. Duane had just finished lighting a small fire in the wood stove to take the chill out of the evening. He whistled as he closed the stove door and opened the damper. Then he walked over to the stereo and put on one of his jazz tapes. They seemed to fill him, and soon he was pretending to play the saxophone along with the music, rocking back and forth, fingers running all over imaginary keys, cheeks puffing in and out as if he were blowing high notes for a huge crowd of fans. Livi quickly jumped up and began singing— nonsense lyrics about a dinosaur that liked to eat school principals for snacks. Tucker came in to see what the commotion was. The phone rang. Duane boogied right over and answered with a laugh: "Good evening! Renfro Jazz Band at your service. Bookings available. We play, you pay!"

The smile had dropped from Duane's face in an instant. His voice went flat as he turned to Livi. "It's for you," he said. "It's your mother."

Tucker and Duane had stood motionless and listened as Livi laughed and talked with a woman neither of them knew anymore. The joy of the music was gone. What had been left was a look of hurt in the eyes—the same look still there at breakfast.

Tucker went back to his seat and forked the last of his scrambled eggs into his mouth. *I know I promised I'd try to be nice to her. And I have been. Well, OK, maybe not as nice as I could be. But I haven't been rude. I've just avoided her as much as possible, that's all. Please don't make me be with her today, Dad. Joe Allen and I are supposed to test our bows and arrows. Deer season for bow hunters opens in just one week!*

"Please help out, Tucker," his father said. "I don't feel comfortable leaving your sister here alone while I work. Besides, she wants to be your friend. She's been telling me every day how wonderful she thinks you are. She's been telling me how your mother wants to get the family back together." He motioned with his hand toward the back porch where Livi sat writing another letter. "She wanted us to talk to your mother last night on the phone. I just didn't know what to say . . . right then." His voice trailed off unsteadily into silence.

Tucker looked down at his reflection in his breakfast plate. The white glaze was smeared with eggs and butter and dotted with toast crumbs. It made him look like an old man. He hadn't known what to say on the phone, either. He had only looked at Livi when she held the receiver out to him, saying, "Here, talk to Mom." He was at a loss for words now, too.

Duane Renfro stood and walked to the sink. He emptied the remainder of his coffee into it. "Please do this for me today," he said, looking out the kitchen window to where Livi sat. "I'll get a regular job soon, and you'll have your Saturdays free. Everything will be better, you'll see."

Tucker reached into his pocket and ran his fingers over the carved Indian chief. *A warrior of The Tribe always honors a promise made, no matter how hard to keep. I must think of this as a test of worthiness— just like the Mandan warriors. Joe Allen and I can practice with our bows later, I guess.*

Tucker looked up at his father, who still stared out the window. *A test of worthiness.* "OK, Dad," he said as cheerfully as possible, "I'll stay here with Olivia."

"I wish you'd remember to call me *Livi*," she said, smiling. "*Olivia* sounds like you're talking to the queen of England, or a movie star or something, don't you think?"

Tucker watched as Livi opened the mailbox and put her new letter to Kentucky inside. *Do you have to write every day? You talked to her last night on the phone. What are you telling her about us? It's driving Dad nuts.* His eyes quickly scanned the envelope before she shut the door. There was something added to the usual Kentucky address he knew so well. *Ms. Kathy Hayden* it said, then in big capital letters beside her name, *ALSO KNOWN AS MY MOM!*

The anger that rose in Tucker's throat came as quick as it was unexpected. He balled his fists as if to fight it back. *"ALSO KNOWN AS MY MOM," it says. Well, she's my mom, too! Why don't I get letters addressed to "Tucker Renfro. ALSO KNOWN AS MY SON?" Why don't I get letters every day that tell me about a great new book she's reading, how the Cincinnati Bengals are doing, what the weather is like in Kentucky, how work is going? She's my mom, and I hardly know what she looks like, how she smiles, what kind of ice cream she likes. All I've got is that one picture she sent two years ago; that and the letters I've saved. Why doesn't she write ME and ask how I'm doing instead of writing OLIVIA to ask about me? Why wasn't that phone call last night for ME? Why hasn't she cared enough to come out here and—*

"Or Olympian!" Livi said excitedly as she put the red flag up on the mailbox. "Get it? Instead of *Olivia* Hayden, what if Mom and Dad had named me *Olympian* Hayden! I'd probably be a great star of the Olympics!"

Tucker stuck his fists in his pockets, trying to

relax them. *I don't need letters or phone calls from Kentucky. Dad and I get along OK by ourselves.*

He looked at Livi. She was still smiling up at him. "Get it, Tucker? *Olympian* Hayden?"

He pushed a half smile onto his face. "Yeah, I get it," he said.

Livi turned her feet back and forth in the gravel of Tamarack Road. "So what do you like to do on Saturdays?"

Tucker realized he had been holding his breath and let it out. He started to shrug. Livi interrupted. "Hey, let's go look at the turkeys," she said. "I really like the one that's as big as a baby hippo—world-record size!"

Tucker looked down the driveway at the turkey pen. "You mean that dumb old turkey? Icarus?"

Livi looked puzzled. "Who?"

"Icarus," Tucker said, impatience showing in his voice. "That's what Dad named the fat turkey, because he thinks he's a big shot now, but come Thanksgiving he's going to lose all of his feathers, just like the kid in the Greek story who flew close to the sun wearing homemade wings. Dad's into all that mythology. He studied it in college."

Livi's eyes widened. "Oh, yeah? Mom likes it, too. She says the sun melted the wax that held the feathers on and Icarus fell into the ocean and drowned." She looked back over at the turkey pen. "Do you have to kill Icarus for Thanksgiving? He's so big! Let's go watch him strut around the pen."

Tucker scowled. "He's just a dumb old—"

"We could go out in the woods, then," Livi interrupted. "That's what you do every day after school, isn't it? I went on that path that goes down to that dried-up creek. Then it just seemed to disappear. Show me where you go!"

Tucker took a step back as if Livi had pushed him. *She almost found the secret place of The Tribe! I can't let her know!* He took a deep breath and waved his hand toward the creek bed, trying to erase the path from Livi's mind. "That trail you're talking about doesn't go anywhere, just to the creek," he said as calmly as possible. "Your first idea was better. Let's go watch that dumb tur—" He forced another smile. "Let's go see what Icarus is doing."

Icarus was staring through the fence of the turkey pen, making angry gobbling sounds at the dog. Maggie, not to be outdone, was looking into the turkey pen and making low growling sounds at Icarus.

"Quiet, Maggie, you're making that big turkey mad," Livi said with a grin, patting Maggie on the head.

Tucker walked idly over to the pen and poked his finger in at Icarus. The big turkey jabbed at it with his beak. Tucker jumped back. "Hey! What's with you, bird?" he said angrily.

Livi laughed. "He must have gotten up on the wrong side of the turkey pen this morning."

Tucker scowled. "Turkeys don't get up on the wrong side of anything. They don't have enough sense to know the difference between one day and the next."

Maggie growled again. Icarus retreated a bit, but gobbled loud and long at her.

"Like to get in there, huh, Maggie?" Livi said. "I'll bet Icarus would run you right out of there. He's big enough."

"No way," Tucker said stiffly.

Livi turned to Tucker. "You think not?"

He looked down at her. "No way," he repeated.

"I don't know," Livi said, "Icarus looks awful mean."

Tucker looked back into the pen. The rest of the turkeys in the flock were in the far corner. Icarus was still eyeing Maggie and gobbling angrily. Tucker reached down and stroked the back of Maggie's head again. *Olivia is as dumb as Icarus. I guess I'll have to prove it to her. Turkeys do NOT chase dogs.*

This one did, though. As soon as Tucker let Maggie into the pen, Icarus came running right for her, wings spread like a banshee. Maggie growled and tried to look fierce. The rest of the dozen or so turkeys in the pen took note and flew up onto the roof of the coop to get away. But Icarus didn't even break stride. Pecking and gobbling in a feathered fury, he kept on coming, and Maggie—intelligent dog that she proved to be—decided to run.

Livi began to giggle. She reached over and nudged Tucker in the ribs. He was watching wide-eyed through the fence. Back and forth in the pen the two animals were going—Maggie with her tail tucked between her legs, the turkey acting as if death would surely come to any trespasser that messed with his flock.

Then the gate somehow got knocked open. Maggie ran into it, jarring it loose while dodging a particularly well-placed jab by Icarus. Both animals stopped and looked at the path to freedom. But it was Maggie who dashed for it first.

Icarus, however, wasn't done with the canine intruder on his turf. With a wild series of gobbles, he sprung into the air, and before either Livi or Tucker could do anything to stop him, the huge bird was riding Maggie's back out into the yard.

Livi squealed and jumped up and down in place, her arms looking a lot like the turkey's wings. She whooped and shouted, "Ride 'em, Icarus! Ride 'em wild!" Tucker stood glued to the ground, blinking to convince himself that what he was seeing was not real.

Maggie knew it was real, though. She headed straight for an old sawhorse sitting by the garage with a bucket of old car parts hanging from one end. Ducking her head, under she went. Icarus caught the crossbeam of the sawhorse square in the chest. The bucket, car parts, and feathers flew everywhere. And Maggie—looking back over her shoulder to be sure the turkey wasn't coming after her for more—careened off the garage, bumped into the old Volkswagen, and shot across the driveway, hurling herself onto the porch.

Tucker walked over to the dazed turkey and stared down at him. He shook his head, then stooped and tried to pick him up. Icarus was so round and fat there was little to get a good grip on, but in two tries Tucker finally heaved the bird off the ground and began staggering back toward the pen. Icarus gobbled once, struggled for a moment, then twisted his neck around and began to examine Tucker's chin closely.

"I think Icarus likes you," Livi said. She had stopped jumping up and down and flapping her arms, and now stood sporting a sly smile.

Tucker stopped and pulled his head back. Icarus followed Tucker's movement, craning his neck forward. Tucker scowled. "Maybe," he said, leaning back even farther, "but I'm pretty sure I don't like him."

Icarus gobbled.

"See?" Livi said. "He's telling you all about it."

Tucker looked at his sister, then back at Icarus. That was when the turkey reached right up and pecked Tucker on the cheek as gentle as a kiss.

"Aha!" Livi burst out. "It's love! True honest-to-goodness turkey *love!*"

Despite obvious efforts to keep it back, a smile fought its way onto Tucker's face. Livi giggled at the sight of it. To his surprise, Tucker couldn't stop himself from doing the same. First her, then him, then her, then him. The giggling kept itself going like a ball down a hill, until they both gave way to the pull of it, brother and sister laughing, wrapped together in silliness for what may have been the first time in their lives.

# 10

Tucker smoothed the feathers of his first arrow, then fit the notch onto the bowstring. *On opening day I will use this bow and this arrow to hunt with Dad.* He shifted his feet slightly, making sure his body was turned at a right angle to his and Joe Allen's target—a bale of hay propped against the big cedar in the clearing. They had gotten it from Mr. Eldridge when they dropped by to see how the barn roofing was going. Duane Renfro, working on Sunday to get the job done, had waved from thirty feet off the ground.

Taking a deep breath, Tucker raised the bow and pulled the string back to his chin. *I will kill the deer with one shot to the chest.* He sighted down the shaft of the arrow. *It will be my final test of skill and worthiness.* Then he released. The arrow blurred across the clearing in an instant and sunk half its length into the hay bale.

"Wow!" Joe Allen yelled. "It worked that time without wobbling back and forth in the air."

Tucker nodded. *I will become a hunter for The Tribe.* "Yeah," he said, "I guess straightening the feathers was the answer. Try yours."

Joe Allen stepped up to the line they had drawn in the dirt. He fit his arrow to the string, raised the bow, pulled, and fired. The arrow flew across the clearing slowly, dragging itself through the air. It hit the big cedar instead of the hay bale and ricocheted off into the bushes. Joe Allen dropped his arms to his sides. "Aw, I give up," he moaned. "I can't get this thing to work right."

Tucker walked over to the bushes and found the arrow. He sighted down the length of it. "I think the problem is in the shaft, not the feathers. It's crooked. Must have warped on you. You're probably going to have to redo it."

"What about the other two?" Joe Allen asked in a tired voice. "None of them fly right."

"You've got time," Tucker said. "Work on them today and we'll try again tomorrow. Just as long as you've got them fixed and have practiced by opening day is all that matters."

Joe Allen walked over to the tipi and sat down on the old blanket. He blew out a puff of air. "I don't know, Tucker, this is a lot of work. I thought this Indian stuff was supposed to be for fun." He ran his fingers through his curly red hair.

Tucker picked up one of his own arrows and prepared to shoot again. "You can do it, Joe Allen," he said. "Just find some straighter pieces of wood this time."

Joe Allen looked at his arrows, then put them and his bow down. His face suddenly brightened. "Hey, did you know I get my clarinet tomorrow? We start sixth-grade band and *I* will get to sit by Jessica Wagner."

Tucker's arrow flew true, again burying itself halfway in the hay bale. He turned back to Joe Allen. "The main deer trail runs right alongside my house in the gully, then crosses Tamarack Road. I'll bet we can find a good place somewhere in there for you to hunt from. You be sure and pick up the hunting licenses this week, OK?"

Joe Allen held up his hands and wiggled his fingers in front of his face. "These look like good clarinet fingers to me. I took your advice and stopped paying any attention to that crazy sister of yours. No more burping contests. No letting her talk me into ruler-balancing contests, either. I got back at her, too. Did she tell you?"

Tucker came over and sat down. *I made a promise to Dad. I shouldn't have told Joe Allen to ignore her.* Tucker picked up Winter Count and started leafing through it. "Tell me what?"

Joe Allen laughed. "How she got her feet caught in the rings out on the playground at school. And she was just hanging there yelling for help."

Tucker's last entry in Winter Count still had the Xs where he had crossed out Olivia's name. He stared at the writing.

"Except all of the kids were already going into the building and nobody heard her except me," Joe Allen continued with a chuckle. "I got back at her. I just ignored her like you said. A teacher finally came out and got her down." He laughed and slapped his knee. "What a snollygoster she is, huh?"

Tucker reached into his pocket and let the carved Indian chief slip into his palm. *She's not that bad. We actually had a good laugh together yesterday. And she covered for me today. She told Dad that she just wanted to stay home and watch the Cincinnati Bengals football game on TV; that I didn't have to stay with her again like I did yesterday. She knew I wanted to do something special, but she didn't get nosy and ask what. She's really not so bad.*

"Or maybe she's worse than a snollygoster," Joe Allen continued. He pulled out his dirty-word list and ran his finger down the page. "Yeah. Look at this one, number nine. How about that one for Olivia?"

Tucker looked at the word, then quickly closed Winter Count and stood. The anger that crept into his voice was a surprise to both him and Joe Allen. "Fix your arrows," he said. "I'm going home."

Joe Allen stood. "Hey, what's the hurry?"

But Tucker had already picked up his bow and arrows and ducked into the tunnel leading out of the clearing—too far away for Joe Allen to hear him mumble words neither of them would ever have predicted: "And don't talk about my sister like that. She's not that bad."

# 11

It was Sunday, and yet the red flag on the mailbox was up again. Tucker saw it as he was crossing Tamarack Road. *So that's what Olivia really wanted to do—sit home and write another letter. She writes a letter no matter what day it is. Probably wanted to tell Mom about yesterday.* He smiled. *That was so funny—a turkey chasing a dog, then giving me a kiss.*

Tucker stopped in the middle of the gravel road and looked at the mailbox. *I wonder what she wrote. What did she say about me?* He glanced over at his house. Other than a light on in the kitchen, there was no sign of anyone. *Did she tell her that I'm wonderful like she told Dad? Did she say I'm a good*

69

*brother? That I help Dad? That I do my best at school?*

A car came around the curve on Tamarack Road. Tucker stepped back by the mailbox and covered his face with his hand so the dust wouldn't get in his nose or mouth. The cloud of grit billowed up between him and the house. He looked again at the mailbox with the red flag up. *What difference would it make if I read just one letter? Just one? It wouldn't be breaking my promise. And I could put it back and no one would ever know the difference. What did she say about me?* He looked again toward his house, as if Olivia needed to hear what he was thinking. *She's my mother, too, you know. You wouldn't mind, now that we're kind of getting along, would you?* Then he took the letter from the box, stuck it in his pocket, and ran into the woods.

Tucker sat down under a pine tree and opened the letter—carefully, hoping he could reseal the envelope. He unfolded the page and began to read.

*Sunday, September 11*

*Dear Mom,*
*Just a quick note today. I want to watch the football game on TV. Do you think I should still root for Cincinnati now that I'm living closer to Seattle? I guess it doesn't matter.*

*What I really like best is watching the instant
replays. Don't you wish you could have them
on Christmas morning? It would be like getting to open each present twice!*

Tucker smiled at the thought of doubling the
number of Christmas presents with video magic.
*That's just like her to think of something like that.*
He read on.

*Tucker and I had so much fun yesterday.
We watched a big turkey named Icarus chase
a dog! It was really funny. Then that turkey
actually kissed Tucker! Can you imagine being kissed by a turkey? Yuck!*

Tucker looked up from the letter, through the
trees and across the road toward his house. *Yuck is
right. It was funny, though, wasn't it?* He went
back to the letter, picking up speed as soon as he
read the next line.

*Tucker is a great brother. He knows so
much about the forest and about Indians and
things like that. He introduced me to his
friend, Joe Allen, too. I told you he even let
me have his room to sleep in while I'm here,
didn't I? Wasn't that neat of him to do that?
He's REALLY NICE.*

Tucker read the last sentence again. *She used capital letters to write REALLY NICE. Boy, if she only knew what I've been thinking about her all of this time, she wouldn't have.* He stuck his hand down in his pocket and felt for the Indian chief. *I shouldn't have been so hard on her for so long. She really isn't all that bad.* He turned back to the letter.

> *Idaho is neat. We can see the mountains from the kitchen window and I even saw a big deer with huge antlers out in the meadow behind the house yesterday evening. It was just like in a movie or something. That deer was so beautiful!*

Tucker nodded to the letter as if Olivia were there instead, actually saying to him what he was reading.

> *Being here with Tucker and Dad is even better than I thought it would be. Wouldn't it be great if we could all live together as a family? Think about it. OK, Mom?*
> *Bye for now.*
>
> > Love,
> >
> > *Livi*

Tucker read the entire letter again, this time more slowly. The last paragraph he read twice more, one particular phrase in it four times. . . . *together as a family . . . together as a family . . . together as a family . . . together as a family.* The words seemed to stand out from the rest of the letter as if they were written in bright red ink. Tucker couldn't take his eyes from them. *Would it be so great? Together? Together as a family?*

Tucker stood. He folded the letter carefully and put it back into the envelope. "Together as a family," he said out loud, testing the words to see how they felt on his tongue.

There was just enough glue left on the envelope flap for it to reseal. Tucker licked it and pressed it shut, then ran quickly out of the woods. He put the letter back in the mailbox, then walked down his driveway toward home.

"Together as a family . . . together as a family." The sound of it felt better each time he said it. Better than he ever could have imagined. He bounded up the steps, a smile growing larger on his lips with every upward motion, reaching ear to ear like his sister's by the time he opened the kitchen door.

It vanished instantly, however, when he saw Livi sitting at the kitchen table. The look in his sister's eyes spoke of nothing but pain. "It's Dad, Tucker," she said in a shaky voice. "I just got a call. He's fallen off the roof of the Eldridges' barn."

# 12

"I want to see my dad," Tucker said nervously. "Why won't they let me see him?"

He and Livi stood in the doorway of the emergency room at Bonner General Hospital. Mr. and Mrs. Eldridge stood behind them in the hall. They had given them a ride into town.

"It's all right, Tucker," Mrs. Eldridge said gently. "They have to fix that leg of his first, you know."

Tucker shifted from foot to foot, trying to see around the curtain where a doctor and two nurses worked on his father. "But are you sure that a broken leg is all that's wrong with him?"

Mr. Eldridge put his hand on Tucker's shoulder. "The fall knocked him out for a few minutes. It was

74

at least thirty feet. Thank goodness I had pushed that old straw out of the barn with the tractor. He fell right onto it."

"But is he going to be OK?"

Livi jumped on Tucker's question before Mr. or Mrs. Eldridge had a chance to open their mouths. "Of course he is!" It was the first thing Livi had said since leaving the house.

They all looked at her. She had inched through the doorway and now stood beside the nurses' station. She was staring hard at the curtain. "Of course he's all right!" she repeated without looking back at them. "That's my dad in there."

Tucker watched her. She continued to stare without blinking, watching the curtain as if she believed she could mend a broken leg just by concentrating, as if she had to do it all by herself or it wouldn't get done.

Reaching in his pocket, Tucker found the carving of the Indian chief. His fingers ran over it like water over pebbles. He took a deep breath, then let it out. *A family together, right?* Then he moved over beside his sister, and they waited for their dad.

# 13

"And a-one, and a-two, and a-three, step, slide, twirl." Livi danced across the living-room floor in time to the jazz playing on the stereo, her ponytail spinning out and above her head in a helicopter whirl. She stopped near Tucker, who sat in the rocking chair watching. Going on point like a ballerina, she then tiptoed back to her waiting "partner"—the vacuum cleaner. A dainty curtsy to the idle machine brought another chuckle from Duane Renfro.

"Livi, you're just as silly as your grandfather used to be," he said from his place on the couch. He reached down and patted the cast on his leg. "Home for only an hour and you've entertained me nonstop, just like he would've done. I remember it like it was yesterday. Pops never missed the chance to get a few giggles out of a captive audience."

Livi turned and curtsied as prissy as she could make it. "Captive audience?" she said. "They can't keep somebody like you flat on your back!"

Duane laughed. "Oh, yes they can. Until you guys get a father with enough sense not to step backward off a barn roof, flat on my back is just where I'm going to have to stay for a while. I had to promise Dr. Lawrence I'd keep this foot up until the swelling goes down. Then I can move around using crutches. It was the only way I could talk him into letting me out of the hospital. He wanted to keep me there overnight for observation. I told him I'd get the best possible observation if I just went home. Little did he know how right I was."

"Aren't you glad you only broke your leg, Dad?" Livi asked, again dancing with the vacuum cleaner. "If you hadn't landed on that pile of old straw, you'd be missing this show right now."

Duane laughed again. "Imagine that, me laid up in the hospital and you delivering one of the great jazz ballerina performances of the century."

"I'm glad you're here," Livi said from the middle of a pirouette. "That hospital wore me out."

Duane let out a long sigh, his face turning thoughtful. "They say that if you think you are dying, your whole life flashes before your eyes; you can see everything you've ever done for as far back as you can remember."

Livi stopped. "You mean like a rerun on TV?"

"Not exactly." Duane chuckled. "More like the highlights of an entire season, I guess." He reached down and traced Tucker's and Livi's signatures on his cast with his finger. "But my whole life didn't flash before my eyes when I fell off the barn roof today. Instead, when I was lying on that hospital table waiting for Dr. Lawrence to set my leg, I gave a lot of thought to just one part of it."

"What was that?" Tucker asked from the rocker.

"You two," Duane said, "and how glad I am that you're both here with me."

"Aw, shucks!" Livi boomed, covering her eyes in mock embarrassment. "Us?" She bounced over and kissed her father on the cheek, then spun around with her arms out. The grin on her face flashed out, then disappeared as she took yet another spin, this time with the vacuum cleaner cord in tow. It wrapped around her ankles, tripping her. She ended up on the floor, facing Tucker. "I guess Dad meant he'd be missing a *hog-tied* ballerina performance if he were still in the hospital. This is about as silly as a turkey chasing a dog, right, Tucker?"

Tucker had been in the rocking chair since they came home from the hospital—just sitting and rocking, watching his family act like a real family. He smiled. "I saw Maggie out by the turkey pen ear-lier. She was probably teasing Icarus about how few days are left until Thanksgiving."

Livi giggled as she tried to unravel the vacuum cleaner cord. "You watch," she said, "Icarus will make a break for it any day now. This is the Wild West, isn't it? He'll become a turkey outlaw, a real desperado!"

They all laughed at this one, imagining Icarus on the run, a tiny cowboy hat perched on his head, a red bandanna for a mask, six-shooters strapped to his fat feathery sides.

Tucker watched as his father tried to give Livi directions on how to get untangled from the vacuum cleaner cord. They were both laughing so much, nothing was getting done. *I really was wrong about Livi. Maybe she should be a member of The Tribe. Joe Allen sure doesn't seem to care about any of it one way or the other.* He reached in his pocket and held the carving of the Indian chief. *A tribe is a kind of family. That's what we'd be. Livi says that Mom is interested in getting the family back together again. In her letter, Livi made it sound so right, like there's really no other way. Family . . . together . . . all of us . . . after seven years.* "Think about it. OK, Mom?" *That's what Livi wrote.*

Tucker stopped rocking. *Together, Mom? All of us? Like Livi wrote to you? I've saved your letters.*

*I've got them memorized. I wanted to talk to you on the phone the other night, but I just didn't know what to say. Maybe you didn't know what to say either, Mom. Maybe that's why you haven't written more, or called. Would it make a difference in what you decide if I wrote to you, too—like Livi? I know I've been bad about that. I always thought it would be siding against Dad if I did. Anyway, I didn't think it was possible that you two could get back together. Dad said that you didn't want to be part of our lives anymore. You just sort of faded away for me. I started to think about you like you were a dream I had had a long time ago, like you weren't real. I didn't want to write to someone who wasn't real. Would it make a difference if I wrote now, Mom? Now that you seem more real again, even living so far away in Kentucky? Now that Dad is trying again, to prove to you that he can make it? Now that we're all here but you? Together, Mom? Is that what we really need?*

Tucker let the Indian chief fall back into his pants pocket, then got up and walked into the kitchen. He went to the cabinet drawer, where everything that didn't have another place was kept, and picked out a pencil. He could still hear Livi and Duane in the living room, Livi giggling and saying something about being too young to have to spend the rest of her life with a vacuum cleaner tied to her ankles.

Duane's chuckle seemed as light and airy as his daughter's mirth.

Tucker sat down at the kitchen table and flipped back in his school notebook until he came to clean paper. He rolled his pencil back and forth in his fingers, then listened again to his father's and sister's laughter. *All here but you.* Then he began:

*Dear Mom . . .*

# 14

It was the following Friday after school before Tucker and Livi could get the pie made. "Fresh huckleberries poured into a ready-made crust," Livi said. "A surprise! Dad will love it!"

The swelling had gone down quite a bit in Duane's leg. He was up and about now, though not a lot. Tucker and Livi had helped him hobble out behind the garage on his crutches. They left both him and Maggie sitting in lawn chairs next to the woodpile, the autumn sun shining warm on them from a crystal-blue sky. Then they had rushed inside and got to work.

"Are you sure he doesn't know what we're doing?" Tucker asked, checking the oven temperature to be sure it was right.

"A complete surprise," Livi said, licking the huckleberry juice from the spoon.

Livi suggested that Tucker alone deliver the pie to Duane when it was done. "That and a fork . . . or two," she said with a smile.

"But you helped make this pie just as much as I did," Tucker insisted.

She picked up a dishrag and began wiping off the kitchen counter. "Yep, and you can bet I'll get a big piece after dinner," she said. "I just want to finish cleaning up here and then write Mom a letter. We've all been so busy, I didn't get to write yesterday."

Tucker stood, pie in hand, and looked at Livi. *I mailed my letter to Kentucky on Monday. That was five days ago. It probably took three days to get there. One day for her to find time to answer. Three days back across the country. That's seven days. I should get a letter from Mom this coming Monday. Livi has been getting one a day. Starting Monday I'll get a letter—*

"Go on," Livi said, shooing Tucker toward the door, dishrag waving. "Don't worry about me and that huckleberry pie. You're forgetting that it's *your* turn to do the dishes tonight. *That's* when I'm going to sit and eat a piece as big as Icarus the turkey!"

Duane and Maggie were still in place when Tucker walked around the garage to deliver the huckleberry pie. The only difference was that they were both staring intently at the woodpile.

"Shhhh!" Duane said without looking up, finger to his lips. "Maggie and I have been waiting a good ten minutes to take a shot."

Tucker craned his neck forward to see what was going on. His father held a squirt bottle in one hand, pointing it at the woodpile. "There's one." He slowly raised the squirt bottle and squinted one eye to aim. "I've found their hideout, and now I'm going to teach those stinkbugs not to invade our house every fall."

"You're shooting at *stinkbugs*?" Tucker asked, pie and two forks in hand.

Duane nodded, the squirt bottle still trained on the woodpile. "Big-game hunting, Tucker!" he laughed. "Lions, tigers, bears, stinkbugs. I just couldn't resist, so I armed myself with this handy bottle of windshield cleaner I'd left out here."

Maggie squirmed on her chair and let out a low growl at the dark gray bugs now crawling out from under the woodpile. Duane took a deep breath, checked his aim again, then with a whoop started squirting. "Yahoo! Take that and that and that, you little stinkers!"

The mixed smells of windshield cleaner and stink-bugs under attack filled the air. Maggie barked. Duane pulled and pulled on the plastic bottle trigger until all of the bugs had retreated back under the woodpile. He chuckled. "You'd think a man with two college degrees would know you can't wash the smell off those things as easy as the grime off a windshield, wouldn't you?"

Tucker laughed. "I hate it when I step on one by mistake."

Duane pinched his nose between a finger and his thumb. "Awful smell, isn't it? Like rotten eggs or something worse." He reached over and patted Maggie on the head. "Stinkbug hunting with a squirt bottle. Only a man with a broken leg would do that, huh, Maggie?"

The smile on Duane's face faded. He looked down at the cast on his leg. The crutches lay on the ground beside his lawn chair. "I'm afraid I won't be able to take you hunting this deer season, Tucker," he said. "I'm sorry."

Tucker stood very still for a moment. Duane looked up at him. Tucker hesitated, as if he had forgotten what he came for, then offered the pie.

Duane reached out and took it, pulling it under his nose and inhaling deeply. The smile returned to his face. "Huckleberries," he said. "I love the smell of them almost as much as the taste."

Maggie jumped from her lawn chair. Tucker slowly sat down in it. *I've been practicing with my bow every day. Tomorrow is opening day. It's my final test of worthiness and skill. I can do it alone. I knew Dad probably wouldn't be able to help. He hasn't been able to help with finishing the bow either. That's OK. He's been busy looking for a job. And now there's his leg. I can do it alone. That's OK.*

Duane stopped sniffing at the huckleberry pie and looked at Tucker. The expression on his face changed somehow, not dropping the smile the pie had brought him, but not holding it either. "Your mother used to make huckleberry pies for me when we first got married. We were fresh out of college, and I was working at my first teaching job. We were in Kentucky then, so she had to use canned huckleberries. But she knew how much I loved the taste and the smell of them right out of the oven. She knew that being back East, so far away from everything I'd grown up with here in Idaho, was hard for me. The pies were like her gift from the West. We were very much in love."

Tucker handed his father one of the forks. *I've been watching and tracking the big buck. I know just where to wait—in the birch tree behind the meadow. I know I can get him. I just know I can. One shot to the chest. My final test.*

"But huckleberry pies don't keep a marriage together," Duane said. He stuck the fork into the center of the pie and cut out a bite. "It can fall apart despite the fact that two people love each other."

Tucker stuck his hand into his pocket and let the carving of the Indian chief slip into his hand. He gripped it tightly. *It's OK now. Everything is going right for me. I'm going to get that big buck tomorrow. It'll be perfect. Only one shot. Mom's letter will get here on Monday. Dad will get a job soon. A tribe! That's what we'll all be. Family! Together! It's going to happen. I just know it! It's GOING to happen!*

On and on he went, gripping his dreams just as his fingers gripped the carving in his pocket— family, the hunt, The Tribe. The images kept coming in seemingly endless streams . . . so fast and free Tucker never gave notice to the tears that had welled up in Duane Renfro's eyes.

Later, on the way home from practicing with his bow and arrows, Tucker stopped at the mailbox. *Livi has probably already picked up today's mail like she usually does. Mom's letter to me isn't due till Monday, anyway. But what harm does it do to just check?* To his surprise, several envelopes lay face-down in the box. He pulled them out and closed the door. The first letter he turned over was from Kentucky. As usual, it was addressed to Livi.

Tucker stood for a moment and looked at the envelope: the stamp with a picture of an old riverboat on it, the handwriting so neat and clear, the name that headed the return address—Kathy Hayden. He looked up at his house. *She's already written me by now, you know, Livi.* He put the letter up close to his face and breathed in deep. The envelope smelled faintly of perfume. *And mailed it, too. It'll be here on Monday.*

Tucker turned the letter over and over in his hand, watching the handwriting appear and disappear. He looked back up at his house. *You wouldn't mind if I read it, would you, Livi? You're always telling me what Mom said in the letters she wrote to you, anyway. It wouldn't matter, would it? My letter will be here on Monday. And anyway, it's from OUR Mom, right?* Then he turned and ran back across Tamarack Road and into the woods, tearing the letter open as he went.

# 15

The cold rain began an hour before dawn on Saturday. At first it was only small patters on the birch and aspen leaves overhanging the clearing. Soon it began to drip to the dry ground, leaving round marks in the dust. It also dripped on the back of Tucker's neck as he tried to light damp twigs in the fire pit. He ignored it, striking one match and then another, his hands moving in quick, jerky motions.

Tearing the last match from the pack, Tucker stopped and took a deep breath. *A hunter for The Tribe must begin by keeping a clear mind.* He struck a match. It lit. He held it under a piece of shredded cedar bark. A thin curl of smoke rose almost immediately. He quickly pushed the match closer, shielding it from the rain with his hand. A small orange flame grew. Getting down on his hands and knees, Tucker blew gently on the fire. It caught the twigs. He put on bigger sticks and blew some more. Flames began to flick upward. Crackling sounds filled the clearing.

Tucker nodded to himself. *Now to start the ritual of preparing for the hunt.* He moved directly into the drifting smoke from the fire and sat cross-legged. Eyes closed, he let it bend and curl around his clothes, his face, his skin, his hair.

Only seconds later a freckled face crowned with red hair appeared in the circle of firelight. Tucker looked up through the smoke. Joe Allen smiled and waved. "Hi."

"Sit down," Tucker said, voice gruff. He closed his eyes again.

The smile fell from Joe Allen's face. He walked over to the fire pit, but didn't sit down. "What's with you?"

Tucker talked without opening his eyes. "We're late," he said, the smoke still curling around him. "It'll be daylight soon. We've got to prepare for the hunt—just like I read the Indians used to do. The smoke will cleanse our spirits, helping us to be worthy hunters, that's what the books say. It will help hide our scent too, so the deer can't smell us. Sit down."

Joe Allen still didn't sit.

Anger crept further into Tucker's voice. He spoke through tight lips, eyes still closed. "The books say the Indians used to play drums and smoke a pipe. It was supposed to give them strength, make a bridge to the sky. It was all part of preparing for the hunt. Now *sit down.*"

Joe Allen finally moved, but only to crouch and rub his hands together. He held them out to the warmth of the fire. "My fingers feel like a tongue stuck on a January flagpole," he said. He continued to hold his hands over the fire. "Hope I haven't got frostbite. The last thing a man in love needs is cold fingers, right?"

Tucker opened his eyes again. He scooted back out of the smoke and looked right past Joe Allen to his bow and arrows. They were in the tipi, still wrapped in the old wool blanket and tied with a leather thong. His small sheath knife lay on top of the bundle. "Have you got the hunting licenses? You said you'd get them in town yesterday."

"Couldn't play the clarinet either, not with fingers like these," Joe Allen went on. "Guess I'd have to settle for growing old by myself with no music."

"Joe Allen!" Tucker almost yelled. "Where are the licenses? This is the day we become hunters for The Tribe. I've already started an entry in Winter

Count about it." He looked closer at his friend. "Hey, where is your bow?"

Joe Allen didn't look away from the fire. "I guess I'd just have to collect dirty words for a living."

Tucker's fist came flashing out in a blur. He hit Joe Allen square in the shoulder, knocking him sprawling. "You didn't bring your bow, did you?" Tucker roared, jumping to his feet. "You didn't get the licenses, either. I was right. You don't care. You aren't one of The Tribe!"

The shock of being hit went out of Joe Allen's face as he too sprang to his feet, fists balled at his side. "Don't hit me unless you don't mind getting hit back."

Tucker didn't back off. "Do you want to be a member of The Tribe or not?"

It was Joe Allen's turn to lash out. "Get off it, will you! This Indian junk is just for fun. It's not real. Don't you know that?"

"Liar!" Tucker screamed. "You're all liars!" He lunged forward. This time Joe Allen was ready for him and jumped to the side. Tucker caught him by the arm. They both went to the ground in a flurry of fists. Tucker swung at Joe Allen's face but missed, catching him only in the side of the head. Joe Allen swung back and hit Tucker in the side. Tucker threw himself onto Joe Allen's chest. They rolled close to the fire. Joe Allen pulled free just in time and scrambled out of Tucker's grip and to his feet. Tucker jumped up and started toward Joe Allen.

"We can't go hunting!" Joe Allen yelled, his breath coming in deep gulps.

Tucker stopped short, trembling with anger. "What do you mean, we can't go hunting?"

Joe Allen ran his fingers through his hair. "My bow doesn't work, my arrows won't fly right, and I didn't get the hunting tags. I couldn't. You were so into this whole Indian thing, you forgot to think about a few Idaho things—like the law that says you have to be twelve years old to get a hunting license, which we aren't yet. And that you can only get a license *after* you've taken a hunter safety course, which we haven't, and *after* you've paid eight dollars, which is more than either of us have."

Tucker narrowed his eyes and took a step forward. "You're lying, just like—"

"No, I'm not!" Joe Allen shot back. "We can't hunt. I've known it for weeks. I wanted to tell you. I just couldn't make myself do it. Come off it, Tucker. You've been living in a dream. You're not an Indian and neither am I. We've just been playing at it. We can't get a deer with these homemade bows and arrows."

Tucker lowered his fists. Stiffly he walked over to the tipi and picked up the bundle containing his bow and arrows. He quickly put the knife on his belt. "Maybe this has all been just a game to you," he said, turning to face Joe Allen again, "but today is as real as it's going to get for me. License or not, I'm going hunting."

Joe Allen looked up at the still dark sky. The rain had picked up even more and was now dripping steadily through the trees. He shook his head. "OK, go then," he said, and walked from the clearing into the predawn woods.

Tucker looked after him for a minute, then turned back to the fire. A look of complete shock came over his face. Livi stood just inside the firelight, hands buried in her coat pockets, collar pulled up around her ears.

"Hi," she began, "I just wanted to know if—"

"What are you doing here?" Tucker demanded, the anger returning to his face in an instant.

Livi stepped back as if pushed. She stumbled over her answer. "I . . . just . . . I heard you get up and leave the house. I saw you carrying your bow and arrows. I followed you. Tucker, I just wanted to know if I could be with you when you go hunting—"

"Be with me!" Tucker yelled. He dropped his bow and arrows onto the ground. Reaching into his jacket pocket, he pulled out the letter from Kentucky. "Just like she'll be with me?"

Livi's eyes grew wide. Anger crept into her voice. "Tucker, is that a letter from Mom?"

He shook it at her. "Yes! It's a letter from Mom."

"That's mine!" Livi blurted out, moving halfway around the fire toward him. "When did it come? What does it say?"

"It says she's not coming, that's what it says."

Livi stopped. "Oh," she said, her voice dropping to a whisper.

Tucker shook the letter at her again. "It says that she has told you over and over again that she and Dad will never get back together; that they would never be able to get along; that she doesn't want to live with a man who can't do anything with his life. It says"—he choked on his words, tears welling up in his eyes—"it says she could never love him again. She probably means me, too."

"Oh, Tucker, no," Livi said.

"YES!" he yelled, shaking the letter at her again, half crumpling it in his fist. "I let myself believe all that talk about Mom wanting to get the family back together. You've been lying to us all of this time. You got Dad to believe it. And you finally got me to, too. I knew I shouldn't have believed you. It was all a lie!"

Livi took another step forward. Tears were running down her cheeks. "It wasn't a lie, Tucker. I wanted more than anything for us to be a family—"

"Stop saying that!" he screamed at her. "It's not going to happen! Go back to Kentucky and leave us alone. You don't belong here. We were doing fine on our own until you came! I don't need a sister! Can't you see that?"

Tucker crumpled the letter into a tight ball and threw it into the fire.

"No!" Livi gasped. She reached into the flames, trying to save the letter. The heat made her pull her fingers back. Smoke billowed around her. She began to cough. She tried to cover her eyes and reach for the letter again. It had caught fire. She finally backed away, coughing and crying at the same time. She stood and looked at Tucker, her face streaked with tears and soot. Her lips stilled for a moment, as if she were about to say something, then began to tremble. Livi turned and, sobbing, ran from the clearing.

Tucker stood, watching the letter burn. Then, without even glancing in the direction his sister had gone, he picked up his bow and arrows in the tipi and walked directly through the path of the drifting smoke and out into the woods.

# 16

Tucker eased over a log and approached the birch tree behind the meadow. There was just enough light to see where he was going, but not enough to pick out any detail on the forest floor. He looked up through the steady rain at the fork in the tree. *I have cleansed myself with smoke. My bow and my arrows are ready. Here is where I will become a hunter for The Tribe.*

The breeze picked up, blowing the treetops back and forth, knocking large splatters of water from the branches. Tucker reached into his pocket and let the carving of the chief slip into his hand. *This is my final test.* He slung his bow over his shoulder, stuck the arrows in his belt, and climbed. *Quiet now, more than ever. A brave must move with all of the skill of a great hunter and keep a clear mind.*

Tucker reached the fork of the tree and looked down. The darkness was quickly giving way to dawn. An open view of the buck's favorite patch of clover lay below. He tried to get more comfortable. The scrape of his jeans on the curly bark of the birch tree made him wince. *But what if the buck heard or saw me coming? Or what if he just doesn't come here today? There are probably lots of places he goes to graze.*

Tucker shook his head, then pushed the wet hair on his forehead to the side. *A clear mind. I have to keep a clear mind.* Taking the bow from his shoulder, he pulled one of the arrows from his belt. He fit it onto the bowstring and sighted down its length. *This is my day. One shot to the chest, using all that I know and have practiced. A true test of skill and worthiness. Alone. I WILL become a hunter for The Tribe.* With a deep breath he pulled his jacket collar up around his ears, and began his wait. *I am ready.*

But Tucker's eyes soon began to roam away from the woods. He gazed between the branches of the birch tree, across the meadow. Although no lights were on, he could make out the outline of his house in the half-light of near dawn, the faint glint of rain on the tin roof, the rectangles of dark windows, in particular his bedroom window. *It's Olivia's fault if*

*I don't get a deer. Things were fine until she came. Now Joe Allen doesn't care about anything anymore except clarinets, Jessica Wagner, and his dirty-word list. And Dad fell off the barn. He could have gotten killed. He was up there because he wanted to show her he could get work, so she'd write good things to Mom about him and then the family would be together again. It was all lies. And we believed it. All lies. Mom never told her that. The only tribe I need is what I have right here in this tree with—*

A muffled snap of a twig underfoot pulled Tucker's attention back. Despite the continued patter of light rain on the leaves and branches, the sound jumped out at him like a cannon going off.

Tucker scanned the area, moving only his eyes. Although it was getting lighter by the minute, the normally sharp lines of tree trunks, logs, and branches were still fuzzy. Nothing moved. Tucker's heartbeat quickened. *My buck is here! I know it!* Still nothing moved or gave itself away with noise. The rain suddenly began to slow. As Tucker listened, it soon faded to only drips from the trees. The quiet increased. Tucker strained his hearing, searching for the sound a hunter needed to hear. Nothing. *Maybe he's not there. I wasn't paying close attention. My mind wasn't clear. It's all her fault. Why can't I forget about her and all of her—*

This time he saw it—a flick of brown and white to

the side and quickly down again. It was a nervous movement, the movement of a deer's tail when the animal sensed something wrong. Tucker held his breath. *Yes! Yes! Yes! Please be him! Please!*

What seemed like forever went by. Then slowly, as if testing thin ice, the buck moved from between two trees. *It's him! He's here!* Three or four steps, stopping still as stone, then forward. The buck moved slowly toward the patch of clover beneath the birch tree. The tail continued to flick out to the side. Flank muscles twitched. Nostrils flared. Ears rotated like radar.

*This is it! I'm going to get my first deer!* He stole a quick glance at his bow and arrow. *But did I fit the arrow in the center of the bowstring? Can I raise the bow and pull the string back without startling him? I can hear my own heart pounding in my chest. Can he hear it, too?*

The buck stood as still as stone again. Tucker slowly released stale breath through his nostrils, paused, and then began to breathe in. *My breath is too noisy. He'll hear it and be gone in a flash. Or Olivia will show up again, sticking her nose where it doesn't belong. Why can't she just go away and stay away?*

The buck dipped his head and took a bite of clover. His antlers—four points on either side—gleamed wet with rain. The tips were white, sharpened on saplings for the fights of the breeding season.

*Look at that! The size of his neck! He looks like a king!*

The massive head came back up, eyes and ears searching the woods for danger. Tucker held his breath again. *He's so close. I'll have to raise the bow and shoot all in one motion. It'll have to happen before he has time to move. Clear mind. Clear mind. One shot to the chest. I will be a hunter for The Tribe. If he would just put his head back down and give me a little extra time . . .*

The buck lowered his head to take another bite of the sweet green clover. Taking another quick breath, Tucker raised the bow, pulled back the string as far as he could, and let the arrow fly.

Zipping through the stillness of the dawn, the fire-hardened tip of the arrow covered the cool, misty distance between Tucker and the deer in a fraction of a second. With a loud thud, it slammed into living flesh and bone. *I got him! In the chest!* The buck wheeled around, trying to sidestep the sudden pain, then reared up on his back legs with a loud grunt, staggered backward, and fell wildly kicking to the ground. The arrow was buried half deep, just behind the front leg. Tucker stood up in the fork of the birch tree, almost losing his balance. *Oh, no! He's still alive. I thought only one shot to the chest would kill—* He watched spellbound as the buck rose, staggered a few steps forward, and crashed to the ground again. Blood, bright red and frothy, blotted the buck's heaving chest as he repeatedly tried to get back up in vain.

Tucker dropped his bow to the ground and slid down out of the tree. He put his hand to his forehead. Sweat was beading on his forehead despite the cool of the morning. His hands were shaking. He held them tightly together for a minute. *Calm down. Calm down. Act like a hunter for The Tribe. Clear mind.* He took a deep breath and picked up his bow and pulled another arrow from his belt. Quickly he fit it to the string, pulled back, and released. The arrow missed completely, sinking deep into the ground near the buck's head. The buck thrashed frantically, grunting and snorting. Tucker tried to swallow and found he couldn't, as if something were blocking his throat. *This is my final test of worthiness. I WILL be a hunter for The Tribe.* He grabbed his last arrow from his belt. It was broken; it probably happened when he slid out of the birch tree. He threw it and the bow to the ground. The buck snorted loudly, bringing more blood to his nostrils. Tucker's breath came in quick gulps of air. Reaching to his belt, he pulled his knife from the sheath. *I WILL BE A HUNTER FOR THE TRIBE.* He took a step toward the buck. The buck raised his head and looked Tucker straight in the eyes for the first time. Blood dripped from his nose onto the wet grass.

"Oh, no," Tucker whispered, his voice trailing off into nothing.

The buck's chest heaved, dark and wet from the wound. He choked, then slowly lowered his head back to the ground. There was a rattling sound from deep inside his body, a gurgling in the throat, then nothing.

Tucker stood for a moment, knife still in his hand. The only noise to be heard was that of his own breath—in and out, in and out, ragged gulps of air that couldn't keep up with the need to breathe. The buck lay motionless. His eyes continued to stare out at Tucker, only now they were lifeless. Tucker dropped the knife and put his hand to his chest.

His heart was pounding. He looked at the buck again—legs crumpled beneath his body, antlers sticking up like dead branches fallen from a tree. Tears began to well up in Tucker's eyes. He brushed them aside. More replaced them. He began to tremble. Then shake. Then he broke. Falling to his knees, Tucker Renfro cried out for the first time in over seven years, a great sob that emptied like water into his cupped hands.

"Tucker?" The voice came from behind him, soft and searching.

Tucker whirled on his knees, almost falling backward. Duane Renfro stood at the edge of the meadow, leaning on his crutches, peering into the woods. The rain had drawn dark streaks on his hunting cap and jacket shoulders. Tucker tried to call out to him, but his voice caught in his throat.

Duane hesitated for a moment, then tried again. "Tucker?" He hobbled carefully into the woods and around the birch tree, feeling his way with his crutches. He saw Tucker. "Ah," he said, "I guessed from talking to Livi that you might be back here. She didn't know exactly where—" Then he saw the dead buck.

Tucker swallowed hard, fighting to keep back the tears. Finally words came out. "I . . . didn't think . . . I didn't think it would be like—" His voice caught again, and he began to cry.

Duane moved closer. Dropping his crutches, he slowly knelt in the wet grass. He looked for a long moment at the arrow in the buck's chest. Then he turned and gently put his hand on Tucker's shoulder. "I know," he said, "it was like this the first time for me, too. I didn't expect the pain. It runs both ways, into the hunter, too."

Tucker wiped the tears from his face with his wet jacket sleeve. His voice came out shaky. "Nothing ever turns out the way I want it to. Nothing!" He raised his hands into the air, then let them drop limp onto his lap. "Why can't something go right for a change, Dad? Why?"

Duane searched Tucker's face with his eyes, then let his gaze wander off into the trees. It was lighter, near sunrise, and the rain had completely stopped. Duane took off his hunting cap and shook the water from it, then put it back on his head, and looked at his son. "Livi told me about the letter from your mother," he said.

Tucker stiffened at the sound of his sister's name. He turned and looked at the buck, and the arrow in his chest. He slowly reached out and touched the white tip of one of the antlers. *I am a hunter for The Tribe. I have passed the final test of worthiness.*

"She also told me about what happened between the two of you this morning, the things that you said," Duane continued. "You really wanted your mother and me to get back together again, didn't you?"

Tucker didn't answer. *I am a warrior.*

Duane let out a sigh. "You want to know why something can't go right for a change," he said.

Tucker kept his hand on the buck's antler. *The Tribe. The Tribe. The Tribe.*

"I guess I've asked myself that same question a million times—especially why something can't go right with your mother and me. But I've always answered by telling myself that it's her fault we aren't all together, that *she* is the one who split us up. I've always blamed her, come up with excuses for myself, just like I've always come up with excuses for everything."

Tucker looked up and started to protest. "No, Dad . . ." The movement he caught out of the corner of his eye stopped him. Through the trees and across the meadow he saw only a short glimpse of Livi walking down the porch steps of the house. She was carrying a suitcase in each hand.

Duane didn't notice. His back was to the house and he was intent on his point. "Yes, I have, Tucker, but now I've finally realized that all the excuses in the world will never make things go right. Me blaming your mother or you blaming Livi won't do it, either. All it will do is push us further apart, stand in the way of things getting better."

Tucker grabbed a quick glance back over Duane's shoulder. Livi was walking down the driveway toward Tamarack Road. He reached into his pocket for the carving of the Indian. Running his fingers over the eagle feathers of the war bonnet, he let them gently fall down onto the face. The carving was so familiar he could picture the chief as clearly as if he had brought it out into the morning light— the high cheekbones, proud chin, distant eyes. Looking back to Duane, Tucker stared. Something had changed, or maybe become more clear. Tucker saw for the first time that the Indian likeness he had carved himself, and held so many times, had the same facial features as his father.

Gathering up his crutches, Duane used them as ladders to pull himself up. "No more excuses," he said with a smile, and offered his hand to Tucker, "how about that?"

Tucker stared at the extended hand for a moment. Then he took it, letting his father—despite the unsteadiness of crutches and a cast—help pull him to his feet.

"Come on," Duane said, giving Tucker a hug, "let's go back to the house. We'll take care of your deer later."

Tucker looked out at the driveway again. Livi was nowhere to be seen. He looked up at Duane. "I'll meet you there, Dad," he said. "There's something I need to do first."

Then he ran across the meadow toward Tamarack Road.

# 17

Minutes later, Tucker was at the creek bed. It was no longer dry. Puddles had collected around the larger rocks. The cracked dirt of summer had turned to mud. Tucker hopped from rock to rock as he crossed, daylight now reaching well into even the deepest thickets of trees.

Once on the other side of the creek bed, Tucker knelt and searched the soggy ground with his fingers. At one point he hesitated, rechecked a small area, then lifted some fallen leaves. A fresh footprint lay beneath. Water was still dripping down the sides. He traced the outline of the track with his fingers, then stood and ducked quietly into the tunnel leading through the brush to the clearing.

Livi was sitting in the entrance to the tipi, a pad of paper in her lap, pen in hand, when Tucker stepped out from behind the big cedar. She jumped to her feet when she saw him, spilling the paper onto the ground. A look of fear came over her face.

"I'm sorry! I know I shouldn't be here!"

Tucker started to speak. Livi stopped him, blurting out her words: "I just wanted . . ." She hesitated and quickly picked up her paper. She stuffed it and the pen into her jacket pocket, then hastily picked up her two suitcases. "I just wanted to leave you a letter." Her voice was apologetic, her eyes looked down. She tried to laugh. "You know how I am about letters."

Tucker nodded. There was a moment of silence.

"I cleaned my stuff out of your room," Livi finally said. "It's just like it was. You can pretend I never came."

Tucker walked over to the fire pit. "I guess you bought a round-trip airplane ticket, huh? Knowing you'd go back?"

She stole a quick glance up at him, then looked down again, but said nothing.

He knelt and poked at the coals. They were cold, drowned in the morning rain. "Mom will be glad to see you."

Her answer came in a near whisper. "Yeah."

Tucker kept poking at the coals. "You didn't tell Dad you were leaving."

She shook her head. "I couldn't make myself say it. So I—"

"Left him a letter," Tucker finished for her.

Livi smiled, but only a small one that quickly faded from her lips. She jiggled her suitcases. "These aren't getting any lighter. I guess I'd better be going or my arms will stretch right down to my feet. I called a taxi to take me to town. I can ride the bus from there to the airport." She moved a few uneasy steps toward the big cedar, sort of scooting sideways, head down. Tucker stood. She immediately turned and started into the tunnel.

"I was mad," Tucker said to Livi's back.

She stopped.

"That's why I said those things earlier."

Livi turned around and faced Tucker. The expression on her face was blank. She started to speak, then stopped, puffing out her cheeks as if they were full of words. When they came, they came in quick bursts. "I just wanted to be your sister, that's all. I just wanted for all of us to be together. You told me to get out of your life."

Tucker shuffled his feet in the wet dirt. "I didn't mean it the way it sounded."

Livi raised up on her toes. "You made it clear from the first day I got here how you meant it. I just didn't want to believe it." She turned back toward the tunnel. "I won't bother you anymore with my stupid jokes and contests and letters. You can have your life back the way you want it. I'll go back to Kentucky to mine."

Tucker stuck his hand down into his pocket and stepped after her. "Did I ever show you this?" he asked.

Something in the tone of his voice made Livi stop and look back. He pulled a small piece of wood from his pocket and held it out so she could see it. It was the carving of the Indian chief.

"I made it myself," he said.

Livi said nothing, only looked up into Tucker's eyes.

Tucker rubbed his fingers over the face of the chief, then back over the carved feathers of the headdress. "And I've got this journal called Winter Court. It's a record of all the important events of my tribe, just like the Indians used to keep on a buffalo skin."

She still looked up at him.

"But a tribe needs more people than just me to really be a tribe . . . like Dad."

Her brown eyes seemed so much like those of a deer.

"And you like to write . . ."

A smile began on her lips.

". . . so I was wondering"—he paused and held the carving of the Indian chief out for her to touch— "if you might be interested in hanging around and helping me with it."

Livi reached out and ran her fingers across the smooth wood of the carving, over the face and the intricate feathers of the headdress. Gently, she touched the palm of Tucker's hand. They both smiled, a smile that soon spread ear to ear. Then they walked from the clearing and headed home.